I0691479

Seoul Searching Adventure

Mysteries, Mishaps, and Missing Artifacts

By Em Green

Legal Disclaimer:

This book is a work of fiction. Any similarities to real persons, living or dead, are purely coincidental. No AI apps were harmed in the making of this book. Maybe some nudging, but the concept, direction, style and tone were all the author's doing.

ISBN 978-1-969310-00-3

Published by Sean O'Leary Books Publications with the collaboration and cooperation of Margins Abound LLC

Visit www.marginsabound.com for more books by Em Green

Author's Note to Readers

Thank you for traveling to Seoul with me.

This story began with a question: What happens when we chase meaning in a place that changes us before we find it?

Every scene — from the narrow market streets to the quiet temple courtyards — was written with respect for the culture, history, and humor that make Korea unforgettable. I hope this book reminds you that adventure often starts with curiosity ... and that sometimes the missing artifacts are pieces of ourselves we left behind.

Em

Prologue: I shine bright, yet beneath me, secrets hide in plain sight. What am I?

Seoul. The city was alive, a vibrant mosaic of tradition and modernity. The hum of motorbikes wove through the chatter of street vendors, while the soft glow of paper lanterns cast shifting shadows over ornate hanok doors. The air buzzed with anticipation, the kind that promises something extraordinary—though no one could yet pinpoint why.

At the Nation Museum's Lecture Room, Historian Park Joon-ho stared at his phone, irritation mounting as his childhood friend and daily nuisance, Kim Dae-hyun's overly raspy voice finally broke through the static.

Dae-hyun's voice crackled through the line.

"Hyung, you're a lifesaver," he said, his words punctuated by a poorly stifled cough. "Seriously, I owe you big for this."

"I haven't even agreed yet," Joon-ho said, adjusting the strap of his satchel and stepping to avoid a grandmother carting a basket of fresh herbs. "Why are you dragging me into your mess?"

"It's not a mess!" Dae-hyun insisted. "It's just... a slight hiccup. You know, the kind that happens when a hardworking tour guide gets sidelined by death's grip."

"You have a cold," Joon-ho said flatly.

"Hyuuuuung," Dae-hyun groaned, dragging the syllable like a child pleading for ice cream. "Just think of it as a way to expand your horizons. Show off that historian brain of yours to a bunch of Latin American tourists. They'll be so dazzled they won't even notice my script is better than your lectures."

"I don't need your script," Joon-ho snapped, already regretting his existence. "And I definitely don't need to explain why you compared the Joseon Dynasty's royal court to modern K-pop."

"That joke kills," Dae-hyun wheezed. "And so will my fever if you don't help me."

Joon-ho sighed, rolling his eye. The scent of fried mandu wafted from a nearby food cart through his office window, taunting his empty stomach. "Fine. But you owe me dinner. And it better involve actual meat this time. Oh, and if the 'highlight' involves a rubber chicken, we're no longer friends."

Camila adjusted the strap of her camera bag as she stepped out of her boutique hotel into the spring sunlight. The streets of Seoul unfolded before her like the opening pages of an unwritten novel, bustling with life and rich with possibility. Visiting Seoul always felt rejuvenating, every time, like an internal clock knew to reset upon arrival.

By midday, she was lost in the chaos of Gwangjang Market, reveling in the blend of sizzling meat, syrupy hotteok, and stacks of colorful hanbok fabric. Her guidebook had recommended restraint when sampling local delicacies, but restraint had never been her forte.

Approaching a food stand piled high with golden jeon, Camila grinned at the vendor. "This smells like it could change my life," she said in halting Korean.

The vendor laughed, his apron streaked with grease and age. "It will," he replied. "But only if you're brave enough to try the spicy ones."

Camila laughed and took a bite, savoring the mix of heat and texture. As she wiped her hands on a napkin, her gaze snagged on something odd: a bright pink rubber chicken perched on a nearby table. She paused, didn't try to understand why or how it got there, she simply snapped its picture.

Meanwhile, Joon-ho was sweating through his impromptu crash course in tour guiding. Dae-hyun's so-called prestigious group turned out to be a hodgepodge of families, overzealous college students, and one grandmother whose camcorder had been trained on his face since they arrived at Gyeongbokgung Palace.

Sticking to facts had been his plan, but Dae-hyun's ridiculous script haunted him. When someone asked about the pond in front of the pavilion, he found himself saying, "Legend has it the water reflects only the truth... and terrible fashion choices."

The group erupted into laughter, but Joon-ho cringed inwardly. He hated gimmicks.

As they moved toward the palace gates, a young woman darted past, balancing a paper tray of odeng skewers. He barely noticed her, too focused on enduring the grandmother's relentless zoom-ins.

That young woman, Camila, didn't notice him either. She was too busy marveling at the ornate rooftops against the blue sky, wondering how something so ancient could feel so alive.

Later, as the sun dipped lower, Camila wandered the art-filled lanes of Insadong. She stepped into a café, the scent of jasmine tea wafting through the air.

At a nearby table, Joon-ho sat hunched over his phone, furiously trying to convince his sick and crazy friend to stop texting.

"Smile more," one message read.

"You're scaring them," said another.

He groaned, setting the phone down just as Camila brushed past, her tea in hand. Neither noticed the other, but the faint scent of her drink lingered in the air between them.

Outside the café, Camila paused, her eyes catching on a stray cat lounging on a nearby rooftop. Its orange-and-white fur glowed in the fading light as it swatted at a bright pink rubber chicken. With one lazy push, the toy tumbled to the ground, letting out a pitiful squeak.

Camila laughed under her breath, shaking her head. "What is it with this city and chickens?"

Across town, Joon-ho's phone buzzed with another message:

"Hyung, where's the chicken? It's vital for the next tour!"

Under the watchful gaze of a rising moon, a groundskeeper at Changdeokgung Palace crouched near the lotus pond. His broom swept away moss, revealing a faint engraving of a phoenix surrounded by five radiating points.

He stared at it for a long moment, his expression unreadable. "It's been years," he murmured before rising and moving on.

Chapter 1: Speak with kindness, and kindness returns; what am I?

The next morning Camila stepped out, an umbrella in one hand and her camera bag slung across her shoulder. The rain hadn't dampened her excitement; if anything, it added to the city's allure. Seoul in the rain felt like a movie set, the streets gleaming with reflections of neon signs and shop awnings dripping with water.

Her first stop was a small bookstore she'd spotted the day before in Insadong. The owner, an elderly man with kind eyes and an encyclopedic knowledge of Korean poetry, greeted her warmly as she ducked inside.

"Back so soon?" he asked in Korean, motioning toward a shelf of calligraphy books.

"I couldn't resist," Camila replied, shaking out her umbrella. "Your shop feels like a secret, and I love secrets."

She spent the better part of an hour browsing the shop, eventually purchasing a slim volume of translated sijo. As she stepped back into the rain, her stomach reminded her that breakfast had been an afterthought.

Joon-ho stared out his apartment window, clutching a lukewarm mug of coffee. The events of the previous day—the tour guide fiasco, Dae-hyun's questionable script, and the group's inexplicable obsession with asking if that tree was featured in a K-drama—lingered like an itch he couldn't scratch.

His phone buzzed loudly on the kitchen counter, breaking the fragile calm of the morning.

"Hyung, I have a brilliant idea," Dae-hyun announced without preamble.

Joon-ho set the mug down and exhaled. "Does this brilliant idea involve me being roped into another one of your jobs?"

"Don't be so cynical! It's barely 9 AM!" Dae-hyun's voice carried its usual blend of charm and chaos. "Anyway, I was thinking. Why don't we combine forces? Your boring historical facts, my comedic genius —together, we could revolutionize the tour industry!"

"You're not serious."

"Dead serious. We'll call it 'Laughing Through History.' Picture this: Goryeo Dynasty reenactments with slapstick comedy! A quiz show where you get slimed if you miss a question about Confucian principles! The possibilities are endless."

Joon-ho closed his eyes and pinched the bridge of his nose. "Are you feverish?"

"Not anymore, thanks for asking!" Dae-hyun sounded far too chipper for someone who had allegedly been dying the day before. "By the way, did you find the rubber chicken? It's essential for the pitch."

"No. And even if I had, I wouldn't tell you."

"Such a buzzkill, Hyung," Dae-hyun sighed. "Well, I'll check back in when you're ready to embrace greatness. Don't take too long —this city needs us."

Joon-ho hung up, his patience officially worn thin.

Meanwhile, at the shop, Camila completely engrossed in all the shelves of books from various historic eras, quietly and swiftly took pictures. She was grateful to the shop owner for letting her do so and she didn't want to overstay her welcome or disturb others.

Her phone buzzed and her editor Valentina's name appeared on the screen.

" Tell me you've found something interesting," Valentina said by way of greeting.

"Good morning to you, too," Camila replied quietly, looking for the door.

"Come on, querida, it's evening for me. Don't make me beg for an update."

Camila smiled as she quietly left the shop. "Still exploring. This city has layers, Valentina. I think I'm starting to see how they fit together, but it's going to take some time."

"Well, I trust you'll dig up something juicy," Valentina said. "And don't forget to stay on theme. Readers want intrigue, mystery, and—"

"Romance," Camila finished dr yly. "Let me guess: 'and maybe a chaebol prince.'"

"I didn't say that," Valentina replied innocently, though her teasing tone betrayed her. "But it wouldn't hurt."

Camila chuckled, shaking her head and noticing a café just a few steps away. "I'll call if I find anything. But for now, I think the city's hiding its best stories."

"Then uncover them," Valentina urged. "I'll be here, waiting for brilliance."

By sheer coincidence, Camila and Joon-ho ended up at the same small café near

Gwanghwamun. She had chosen it for its cozy atmosphere and the promise of excellent bungeoppang, while he had come seeking refuge from the incessant buzzing of Dae-hyun's texts.

They sat at opposite corners, each engrossed in their own thoughts. Joon-ho's was a spiral of professional crises—a conference paper deadline, and the nagging feeling that his career had hit a plateau.

Camila, on the other hand, was mapping out her following day, scribbling notes in the margins of her guidebook. Her handwriting, slanted and elegant, filled the page with observations like, "Find the best kimchi jjigae in Jongno" and "Research that statue from Bukchon—it felt... important?"

At one point, their gazes briefly met when the barista almost tripped trying to escape the smiles of several young girls quite interested in the coffee prince. Camila laughed softly, while Joon-ho sighed and muttered something under his breath.

Neither thought much of the moment.

As the rain eased into a drizzle, Joon-ho left the café with a renewed determination to get through his to-do list without further interruptions from Dae-hyun. He had just crossed the street when he felt his phone vibrate again.

It was a text, predictably, from Dae-hyun:

"Hyung, I need you to stop by that antique bookstore in Insadong. The owner owes me a favor, and I left something important there last week. Don't ask what it is—just pick it up. Trust me."

Joon-ho groaned but turned back toward the bus stop.

Joon-ho entered the shop, his eyes scanning the shelves for any sign of whatever ridiculous item Dae-hyun had left behind.

"Excuse me." Joon-ho, seeing the man by the counter, approached. "Excuse me, do you have anything left behind by a... very annoying comedian?"

The owner chuckled. "You must be Dae-hyun's friend."

Joon-ho winced. "Unfortunately."

As the doorbell chimed to welcome another customer, the owner handed Joon-ho a carefully wrapped package.

"Your friend is strange, but loyal," he said.

Joon-ho unwrapped it enough to see the item inside and froze.

It was the rubber chicken.

Chapter 2: Though I'm many, I am nothing until strung together; what am I?

The next morning, Camila reclined on her hotel bed, going through the previous day's photos on her tablet. One particular image caught her attention—the bright pink rubber chicken, perched absurdly atop a stack of encyclopedias at the Insadong bookstore. She saved the image for her blog, a bemused smile playing on her lips as Valentina's voice rang in her head: "Chase the weird things—they always make the best stories."

Joon-ho sat in his small office, staring at the glittery pink rubber chicken that Dae-hyun had insisted on involving in his latest harebrained idea. The absurdity of it all gnawed at him, but he couldn't shake the nagging feeling that there was more to the day's encounters than met the eye. He sighed heavily, grabbed the chicken and headed out.

Joon-ho found himself trudging toward Han River Park, clutching the ridiculous chicken in one hand and a growing sense of resignation in the other. Dae-hyun had roped him into yet another scheme—help Dae-hyun practice for a stand-up comedy routine at an open mic night. The excuse this time was supposedly it was to be their contribution to charity.

Meanwhile, Camila wandered the park with her camera, capturing the interplay of sunlight on rippling water and children flying vibrant kites against the backdrop of Seoul's skyline. She paused near a small outdoor stage, drawn by the sound of nervous laughter and scattered applause. Curiosity didn't take long to draw into the main room.

"Ladies and gentlemen," the emcee announced, "please welcome our next act: Kang Dae-hyun and Park Joon-ho!"

Camila froze mid-step. The last name sounded familiar. She was sure she'd heard it somewhere before and the man who stepped onto the stage—clutching a microphone and a pink rubber chicken—was unmistakable.

Joon-ho adjusted his glasses and cleared his throat. "Annyeonghaseyo. Park Joon-ho is my name, this is Kang Dae-hyun, and I'm... not supposed to be here."

The crowd chuckled politely, their curiosity piqued.

"I'm actually a historian," he continued, "so naturally, my friend here thought I'd be great at stand-up comedy. Because nothing says 'funny' like centuries-old dynasties and Confucian principles."

Camila watched with a mix of amusement and secondhand embarrassment as Dae-hyun introduced himself with the ease of someone familiar with getting attention. He then pulled out and handed Joon-ho the rubber chicken.

" This," he deadpanned, "is apparently the secret to enlightenment. According to my friend, it was used in ancient Korea to resolve disputes among scholars. I think the idea was to make them laugh until they forgot why they were arguing."

The crowd's laughter grew, and even Camila couldn't suppress a grin. She raised her camera, capturing the moment as

Joon-ho's awkward charm slowly won over the audience.

After the performance, Dae-hyun practically dragged Joon-ho off the stage, his enthusiasm as boundless as ever. "Hyung, I was amazing! I told you The! The chicken was a hit! Oh and you were good. The best straight man I've ever had. "

"I'm the only straight man you've ever had and it was a disaster," Joon-ho muttered. "And I'm never doing this again. I was held hostage by your chicken."

Before Dae-hyun could argue further, a deep, melodic voice cut through the chatter.

"Now, that was something I wasn't expecting to see in my club."

Both men turned to find Preston Gregory leaning against the bar, his arms crossed over his broad chest, a knowing smirk playing at his lips.

Dae-hyun brightened instantly. "Ah! Preston-hyung! How's my favorite American-'totally Korean in another life' business mogul?"

Preston chuckled, shaking his head. "The way you butter people up, I don't know whether to be impressed or worried." He clapped Joon-ho on the shoulder, his expression softening slightly. "Joon-ho. Been too long."

Joon-ho exhaled, his tense demeanor easing just a fraction. "It has. Apologies that the museum takes up more of my time now."

Preston grinned. "I get it, it's where your heart is at. You still have that way of making everyone feel like they've walked into a history seminar. You should consider going out more."

Dae-hyun threw his hands up. "Exactly! That's what I've been saying! I mean if he's not even going to attempt to be dating then at least his comedy could use a little flair—maybe a song, some interpretive dance—"

Joon-ho shot him a look that could have frozen boiling water.

Preston, ever the diplomat, raised his hands in mock surrender. "To be fair, you two work surprisingly well together. I'd pay to see that again."

Dae-hyun perked up. "Really? Because I am looking for—"

"No," Joon-ho cut in.

Preston chuckled again. Joon-ho turns to his uni friend.

"Preston, do you ever miss the States? Ever think about running a nightclub back home? I hear the Smithsonian is looking for people."

Preston shook his head chuckling. "Not really. The community here embraced me. This is home now."

Dae-hyun interjected with a grin. "Well, it helps that you speak and sing like a native. Very few can channel Lee Moon-sae's 'Old Love' the way you can."

Preston's eyes widened slightly, and he glanced around the room. "Shh! Don't mention that song too loudly. If the patrons are reminded, they'll insist I sing it over and over."

Dae-hyun laughed. "Can't blame them. Your rendition is legendary."

Preston sighed, though a smile tugged at his lips. "This is precisely why I don't invite you to perform here often. You instigate too much drama."

Dae-hyun feigned offense, clutching his chest. "Me? Instigate? Never!" He squeezed his rubber chicken, which let out a comical squeak.

Joon-ho rolled his eyes. "And this is why I can't take you anywhere."

At that moment, Preston's gaze shifted, noticing a woman observing them from a few feet away. Camila had been quietly studying the trio, her journalist instincts buzzing. There was an undeniable respect between Preston and Joon-ho, a stark contrast to the chaotic banter she'd just witnessed between the historian and his best friend.

"You must be a first-timer here," Preston said, flashing his signature easy-going smile.

Camila arched a brow. "That obvious?"

Preston leaned against the bar, giving her an appraising look. "I make it a point to know my regulars. New faces stand out."

Dae-hyun wiggled his eyebrows. "And here I thought it was my comedic genius that got her attention."

Joon-ho groaned. "I will literally pay you to stop talking."

Camila grinned at their antics but turned her attention back to Preston. "You own this place?"

Preston nodded. "Ten years and counting."

She tilted her head, curiosity flickering in her eyes. "An American running a nightclub in Seoul? How did that happen?"

Before Preston could answer, Dae-hyun clapped his hands together dramatically. "Ah! Excellent question, dear guest! You see, our very own Preston-hyung is not just any expat—he is a Seoul legend!" He gestured grandly, as if presenting an exhibit. "A man of mystery, a voice smoother than aged soju, and a business mind so sharp it could slice kimchi paper-thin!"

Preston sighed, shaking his head. "And this is exactly why I never let you tell my story."

Dae-hyun ignored him, turning to Camila with exaggerated enthusiasm. "He was embraced by the people, not just because of his incredible knowledge of Korean history and culture but also because the man sings like an angel that once dated a trot singer and a K-drama lead at the same time."

Preston held up a hand before Dae-hyun could add more. "Let me stop you before you start claiming I invented K-pop." His lips twitched into a small smile as he finally met Camila's gaze. "The truth is simpler. I was an exchange student that fell in love with the culture, and Korea became home. And when a place treats you well, you find ways to stay and give back."

Something about his tone made Camila even more intrigued. "I get the feeling there's a story there."

"There are many stories," Preston said smoothly. "Some I tell, some I don't."

Before she could press further, Dae-hyun clapped his hands together. "And speaking of stories—our next act!"

Joon-ho groaned audibly. "I am not doing this again."

Camila chuckled. "I think I'll stick around for a bit longer. This place is starting to get interesting."

Preston gave her a knowing look. "That it is."

Camila watched him for a moment, intrigued by the weight behind his words. Dae-hyun, however, exhaled dramatically. "Ugh, hyung, that was so boring. You should have let me finish!"

Preston smirked. "And again, that is why you don't get invited to perform here often."

Dae-hyun gasped, clutching his chest. "Et tu, Preston?" He squeezed his rubber chicken, which let out a pitiful squeak of sympathy.

Joon-ho turned to Camila, his expression a mix of recognition and reluctance. "Have we met? I've seen you around Insadong."

"Guilty," Camila said, smiling. "I couldn't help but notice your... unique choice of prop."

Dae-hyun grinned, extending a hand. "Kang Dae-hyun, comedian extraordinaire and curator of chaos. And you are?"

"Camila Luzardo Rios," she replied, shaking his hand. "Photojournalist and accidental observer of whatever this is."

"It's destiny," Dae-hyun declared.

Joon-ho groaned. "It's nonsense."

"Not much of a comedian, I take it?" Camila asked.

"Definitely not," Dae-hyun said with a laugh. "But he's got an eye for things that matter. Cultural stuff. Legends. Artifacts." He lowered his voice dramatically. "Mysteries."

Intrigued, Camila took a seat. "Mysteries, huh? Sounds like my kind of stor y. Care to share?"

Joon-ho sighed, clearly reluctant, but Camila's curiosity and Dae-hyun's charm kept the conversation going. They chatted for a while before Dae-hyun suggested they move somewhere quieter.

Preston, who had been listening with mild amusement, checked the time and pushed himself up from his seat. "As much as I'd love to hear what trouble you three are about to get into, I've got a business to run." He gave Joon-ho a firm nod. "Good to see you again, my friend. Don't be a stranger."

Dae-hyun smirked. "Oh, before you go, Preston-hyung—should I tell our new friend here about your legendary rendition of 'Old Love'?" It was obvious by how loudly he asked, that Dae-hyun was looking for trouble.

Preston froze mid-step, slowly turning his head toward Dae-hyun with a look that promised consequences.

The damage, however, had already been done. A few nearby patrons perked up at the mention of the song, their eyes lighting up in recognition.

"Wait—Preston, you have to sing it!" one of them called.

"Come on, you know you're the best at it!" another chimed in.

Preston inhaled deeply, his jaw tightening. Then, with the patience of a man who had endured far worse from Dae-hyun, he made a subtle slicing motion across his throat—a silent but clear cut it out gesture aimed squarely at the grinning comedian.

Dae-hyun wiggled his eyebrows, clearly enjoying himself far too much.

With a resigned sigh, Preston strode over to the eager table, offering them a warm smile as he casually picked up a menu. "How about another round on the house instead?" he offered, expertly steering the conversation away from the stage.

The patrons murmured amongst themselves, momentarily distracted, and Preston shot Dae-hyun one last warning glance before heading toward the bar.

Dae-hyun, victorious, leaned back in his chair. "It's the little things in life."

Camila's phone buzzed in her pocket. Valentina's name lit up the screen, and she excused herself and stepped aside to answer.

"Tell me you're uncovering a stor y," Valentina said without preamble.

"Not sure yet," Camila replied, glancing back at Joon-ho and Dae-hyun with a curious smile. "But I think I've stumbled across some interesting people."

Moments later, Joon-ho received an urgent call from the curator at the National Museum.

"Park, we've uncovered something that might be tied to the Path of Five Virtues. We need you to examine it immediately."

Camila, overhearing part of the conversation, tilted her head curiously. "The Path of Five Virtues? What's that?"

Joon-ho hesitated but finally relented. "It's an ancient legend about five artifacts representing Korea's core values: loyalty, honesty, bravery, respect, and kindness.

Supposedly, when brought together, they lead to... enlightenment. Or so the stories go."

Camila's eyes lit up. "Sounds like a story worth capturing. Any chance I could come along?"

Before Joon-ho could respond, Dae-hyun piped up from across the room. "Oh, I'm coming too! A historic discovery needs a guide, right? Plus, the historian package comes with jokes. No extra charge."

On the phone, the curator paused as Joon-ho hesitated. "If you're with trusted company, it might not hurt to bring them along. It could give you plausible deniability if anyone asks why you're involved. Just make sure they don't complicate things."

Joon-ho considered the suggestion, then glanced at Camila. Her expression was unusually serious, and for reasons he couldn't quite articulate, he felt reassured. In a moment of pure instinct, he agreed.

"Fine," he said slowly to the two, looking way too enthusiastic for him. "But no interfering."

Chapter 3: Through struggle I grow, and at the end, I bring joy; what am I?

The café near Bukchon Hanok Village buzzed with quiet conversations, the clinking of cups blending with the faint hum of the city beyond. Camila sat by the window, her camera poised and ready in one corner, while Joon-ho had the other end of the table cluttered with notebooks, guidebooks, and a melting iced Americano. They were engrossed in planning their next stop when a voice behind them cut through their concentration.

"Bukhan Mountain?"

They turned to find Dae-hyun hovering nearby, holding a steaming cup of coffee.

He had spotted the map Camila had spread across the table and couldn't resist injecting himself into the conversation.

"You're planning a hike to Bukhan Mountain?" he asked frowning, his eyes briefly scanning the table for snacks.

Camila nodded. "We are. I've read that there's an old pavilion with beautiful carvings up there. It could be a great place to start. And you're late."

Joon-ho hesitated for a fraction of a second before nodding. "The trails can be tricky. I've hiked that area before—and Dae-hyun can never resist making an entrance."

Dae-hyun leaned back in his chair, tossing the rubber chicken onto the table for dramatic effect. "Hey, looking this good takes time, Hyung. Maybe invest in some sunscreen and stop scowling."

Joon-ho shot him a warning look but chose to stay silent, finally sipping his now weak Americano.

Camila chuckled, turning to Joon-ho. "So, you're a historian and a hiker? Not exactly what I expected."

Joon-ho shrugged. "Something like that," he replied vaguely.

Before Camila could ask more, the sound of the cafe door creaking open drew her attention. A woman stepped inside, her polished yet practical look making her stand out. Camila's face lit up in recognition.

"Valentina?" she called, half surprised.

The woman, carrying a leather satchel over her shoulder, gave a small wave and walked over with a smile. "Don't sound so shocked, Cam. You know I can't resist when you drop words like 'legend' and 'artifacts.'" She glanced at the others, her professional demeanor slipping slightly into curiosity.

"You could've given me a heads-up," Camila said, standing to greet her editor with a brief hug.

"And ruin the element of surprise?" Valentina teased. She turned to Joon-ho and Dae-hyun. "So, these must be the illustrious companions you hinted at in your text."

Dae-hyun was quick to rise, bowing slightly but with his signature flair. "Dae-hyun, at your service—historian, comedian, and occasional hero." He gestured toward Joon-ho. "And this is Joon-ho, the serious one."

"Huh. Valentina Del Castillo Cortez," she introduced herself, extending a hand to Joon-ho instead. "Camila's editor, occasional travel companion, and full-time miracle worker." Dae-hyun was silenced by the gesture but intrigued.

Joon-ho hesitated but shook her hand, his gaze briefly flicking to Camila. "I didn't realize this was turning into a team effor t."

Valentina arched a brow. "Don't worry, I'm just here to make sure Camila doesn't run off chasing shadows. But I wouldn't mind hearing more about this adventure she mentioned."

Camila smirked. "Well I'm glad you're here."

Joon-ho began to gather everything from the table. "Well, now that everyone has introduced themselves, it's time to go."

The hike to the pavilion was a lively affair, with Dae-hyun turning every hill into a stage for his antics. Camila laughed easily at his jokes, while Valentina, ever the pragmatist, challenged his tall tales with sharp remarks that left him scrambling for clever comebacks.

Joon-ho kept to the front, his focus on the trail and the weight of what lay ahead. The addition of Valentina had shifted the dynamic, but her sharp eye and calm energy balanced the group in an unexpected way.

"You climbed this mountain during a storm?" Valentina asked, her tone dripping with skepticism.

"Barefoot," Dae-hyun replied.

"And yet, here you are, unable to climb a hill without complaining," Valentina countered.

Camila stifled a laugh as Joon-ho kept his focus on the trail ahead.

When they finally reached the pavilion, its weathered beauty left them momentarily speechless. The ancient structure sat nestled against the forested hillside, its wooden beams worn smooth by centuries of wind and rain.

"This place is incredible," Camila murmured, stepping back to frame the pavilion in her camera lens.

"It's old," Joon-ho corrected, though his tone betrayed a faint reverence. He began circling the structure, scanning for any signs of significance.

Valentina ran her hand along one of the beams, her editor's eye catching the intricate carvings hidden in the shadows. "These markings—they're deliberate. Could be symbolic."

"Symbolic or not, they're beautiful," Dae-hyun added, leaning casually against a post. "But we didn't hike all this way just to admire the scenery. Where's the excitement?"

Joon-ho sighed. "This isn't a treasure hunt, Dae-hyun. We're here to study, not—"

Before he could finish, Dae-hyun shifted his weight, causing a faint creaking sound beneath his feet. Startled, he stepped back.

"Wait," Camila said, lowering her camera. "Do that again."

"What? Nearly fall through the floor?" Dae-hyun asked, eyebrows raised.

"Just step back there," she instructed.

Reluctantly, Dae-hyun moved back, and the faint creak echoed again. Camila crouched, angling her camera toward the floorboards. "Look here. There's something unusual about this panel—it doesn't match the others."

Valentina knelt beside her, studying the area closely. "She's right. It looks like it was replaced more recently than the rest of the structure."

Joon-ho joined them, carefully running his fingers over the uneven surface. "It could be an access point. Something hidden beneath."

Dae-hyun straightened up with a grin. "See? This is why you bring a comedian along. Accidental brilliance."

"Brilliance or clumsiness, it worked," Valentina quipped, stepping back as Joon-ho retrieved a small tool from his bag.

Together, they worked to gently pry the loose panel free.

Joon-ho took out a tool and carefully pried out the loose panel, the wood groaning softly as it shifted. Beneath it was a shallow recess filled with dirt and small stones.

"That's... anticlimactic," Dae-hyun muttered, crouching beside him. "No scroll, no hidden treasure? I'm disappointed."

"It's not about treasure," Joon-ho said, brushing away the debris. His hand paused as his fingers grazed something smooth and cool beneath the dirt. "There's something here."

The group leaned closer as Joon-ho carefully unearthed a flat piece of what appeared to have once been a polished stone, etched with faint symbols and what appeared to be a feather motif.

"What is that?" Camila asked, snapping a quick photo as Joon-ho lifted the stone into the light.

"Why carve symbols?" Valentina said, studying the faint carvings. "Then hide it?"

"Possibly a way to secretly communicate," Joon-ho replied, turning the stone over. On the back, an even fainter inscription came into view. "This script... it's similar to what's on the pavilion's beams. It could be a key,or a clue to something for those meant to find it."

Camila shone her flashlight on the stone, angling it to reveal the worn text.

"What does it say?"

Joon-ho slowly pondered. "The words are hard to make out, but this line here —'shadows meet where feathers rise'— sounds like a clue."

Valentina tilted her head. "Shadows meeting... that could mean a lot of things. A specific time of day, maybe?"

Joon-ho nodded. "It could be a reference to how light interacts with this place— shadows shifting as the sun rises or sets."

Camila studied the pavilion, her gaze tracing the patterns of the beams and how they aligned with the surrounding landscape. "The way this structure faces east... it's meant to catch the morning light. That has to be significant."

Valentina pointed to a distant grove just beyond the pavilion. "If the sun rises there, it might cast shadows toward this spot. That could be what the inscription is describing."

Joon-ho considered her suggestion, his mind piecing together the details. "It's possible. If we can figure out where the shadows fall at sunrise, we might find the next clue."

Dae-hyun grinned. "So, an early morning stakeout? Sounds fun. I'll bring coffee."

Camila smirked. "Or we could figure it out now—without the coffee." She crouched down, snapping more photos of the stone and the beams. "If we can recreate the way the light moves here, we might not have to wait until dawn."

"Good idea," Valentina said. "We'll need to account for the sun's current position, though."

With Joon-ho's guidance, the group worked together to map out how the sun would rise over the pavilion. Camila's photos helped identify the angles of the beams and the carvings' orientation.

As they spoke, Dae-hyun wandered over to one of the wooden beams, idly tapping it with a twig. "You know, the carvings on these things are pretty wild," he said, half to himself. "I don't know what they mean, but they all point outward, like they're trying to lead you somewhere."

Camila turned toward him. "What do you mean, point outward?"

Dae-hyun shrugged. "I dunno. Just look ." He gestured vaguely at the carvings.

"They're all slanted, like they're pointing away from the pavilion."

Joon-ho frowned, moving to inspect the beams. His eyes followed the faint grooves, realizing Dae-hyun was right. Each line and feather motif angled toward the same direction—the grove.

"That's it," Joon-ho said, his tone sharper now. "The beams are designed to draw attention toward the grove. The sunrise would illuminate the carvings, making it obvious for anyone standing here."

Valentina crossed her arms, nodding slightly. "It's subtle. If you weren't looking closely, you'd miss it. But it's deliberate."

Camila grinned faintly, lifting her camera for another shot. "And here I thought your jokes were your only redeeming quality," she teased Dae-hyun.

Dae-hyun grinned back. "I'm full of surprises."

The group made their way to the rock formation, the sun now sitting at its midday peak. The heat was palpable as they climbed over uneven ground, finally reaching the spot Camila had identified.

Dae-hyun was the first to notice something unusual. "Hey, look at this." He pointed to a faint carving on the side of one of the rocks—a feather, similar to the ones on the beams of the pavilion.

Valentina ran her fingers over the carving, noting the precision of the lines. "It matches the motif on the stone we found."

Joon-ho examined it closely. "There's another inscription here."

He read aloud: "'Where light breaks, the path begins.'"

Camila frowned. "Another riddle."

"Not a riddle," Joon-ho said. "A direction. This is guiding us to the next step."

Joon-ho traced a finger over the markings. "These look like coordinates," he said, glancing at the mountain peak.

It was Valentina who nodded. "It's pointing somewhere higher up the mountain." She chuckled, almost to herself. "Dated a sailor once... okay, maybe twice."

Dae-hyun started to say something, turned slightly red, then stayed quiet.

Joon-ho carefully rolled up the scroll, his mind racing. He couldn't ignore the artifact connection any longer, but sharing that information felt premature. "It could be worth checking out," he said finally, keeping his tone neutral.

"An adventure!" Dae-hyun declared, raising his twig in a mock toast. "Just what we needed."

Valentina smirked. "You're awfully enthusiastic for someone who tripped over every root on the way here."

Dae-hyun grinned. "It's all part of my charm."

Joon-ho glanced at the map again, his expression unreadable. Whatever lay ahead, he knew the next leg of their journey would bring them closer to learning more about the secrets tied to the Path of Five Virtues.

The group set off again, Dae-hyun leading the way with his twig held high like an explorer's staff. The trail narrowed as they ascended, the forest thinning to reveal rocky outcroppings and scattered patches of wildflowers.

"Higher up the mountain," Valentina said, glancing at the coordinates Joon-ho had sketched from the scroll. "I hope you realize this is starting to feel like one of those treasure hunt stories."

"Except there's no treasure," Joon-ho replied tersely, keeping his eyes on the trail.

"That's what people always say before they find the treasure," Dae-hyun quipped, earning an amused glance from Valentina. Dae-hyun reddened but was pleased.

The climb grew steeper, forcing them to focus on the path ahead. As they reached a plateau, Joon-ho paused, his gaze locking on a cluster of stones arranged unnaturally in a semi-circle. Usually stones are placed vertically in a tower. These weren't.

"This might be it," he said, gesturing toward the stones.

The others gathered around, studying the arrangement. Camila knelt to examine the carvings etched faintly into the bottom of the rocks, her camera clicking softly as she captured the details.

"These symbols look like they align with the ones on the pavilion," she noted, glancing at Joon-ho.

"It's deliberate," Joon-ho agreed. "This isn't just a marker—it's pointing to something else."

"Something else that's... buried?" Dae-hyun ventured, gesturing to the moss and dirt covering the center of the semi-circle.

"It's possible," Valentina said, crouching beside Camila. "This placement looks like it could've been a hiding spot for something small—something meant to last."

Joon-ho knelt as well, brushing away the dirt. His fingers caught on a smooth surface, and with some effort, he pulled out a silk-wrapped bundle.

Camila leaned in, her breath catching as she snapped another photo. "Is that another artifact?"

"Not just an ar tifact," Joon-ho murmured, carefully unwrapping the bundle to reveal an aged scroll. The material was delicate but intact, its surface covered in intricate writing and detailed illustrations.

Valentina arched a brow. "That looks ancient."

"It is," Joon-ho confirmed, his tone grave. "And it ties directly to the staff we found at the museum. It appears this scroll may be a part of the same stor y."

The group descended the mountain, the discovery still fresh in their minds. The late afternoon sunlight filtered through the trees, casting long shadows on the trail. As they neared the base, they noticed a man standing in the clearing ahead, his gray hair tied back and his posture calm but alert.

"Ah, there you are," he said, his voice resonant but warm.

Joon-ho stopped abruptly, recognizing the man. "Professor Im?"

Professor Im Hye-won nodded, a faint smile on his face. "I had hoped you'd find something. The curator mentioned your trip. I decided to come see if I could be of help. It seems you came with assistance." He turned to the others.

"Im Hye-won," he said, bowing slightly. "Advisor to the museum and a long-time student of the Path of Five Virtues. It seems you've made remarkable progress." His eyes shifted to the scroll in Joon-ho's hands. "May I see it?"

Joon-ho handed it over. Professor Im unrolled the scroll with care, his expression becoming more serious as he read.

"This confirms it," he said after a moment. "The staff is part of a greater puzzle. And this scroll provides a crucial piece—a map, of sorts, to the next step."

"Next step?" Camila asked, her curiosity piqued.

Professor Im rolled the scroll back up, handing it to Joon-ho. "For now, the curator and I will need to study this further. But this journey is far from over."

As the group reached the train station, they began discussing their next steps.

"I'll take the scroll to the museum first thing tomorrow," Joon-ho said. "The curator and I will need to analyze it."

Dae-hyun stretched with exaggerated drama. "And I've got a city tour lined up— time to wow some tourists with my comedic genius."

Camila smirked. "Try not to trip over your own jokes."

"Part of the charm," Dae-hyun shot back, winking.

Valentina turned to Camila as the others moved ahead to seats on the train. "We'll start drafting the article tonight. But before we publish anything, we'll need the museum's approval."

"I agree. I'll ask Park Joon-ho when we have a moment ," Camila agreed. "It's too important. Plus, collaborating with the museum will give the story more depth."

"Not to mention more access to your handsome historian," Valentina added with a wink.

"I'm not you Valentina. Always trying to find a prince charming. One day, you're going to end up finding a frog that sweeps you off your feet. Then what?"

Valentina shuttered at the thought. "Oh no. You'll have to push me into the nearest volcano then."

As the group parted ways, the weight of their discovery lingered. The scroll was a tangible link to the mysteries of the Path of Five Virtues, and each of them felt the pull of what was yet to come.

For now, they had a plan. Tomorrow, the journey would continue.

Chapter 4: Though I am small, gather enough of me, and I will rise; what am I?

The late afternoon sun filtered through the tiled roofs of Bukchon Hanok Village, casting intricate patterns of light and shadow along the cobblestone streets. Camila meandered through the alleys, her camera poised to capture the interplay of tradition and modernity. Every so often, she paused to jot notes in her journal—observations about the architectural details, the hum of vendors' chatter, and the quiet whispers of tourists marveling at Seoul's blend of past and present.

Not far behind, Valentina strolled at a more leisurely pace, occasionally stopping to admire the hanok architecture. She didn't speak Korean, but her editor 's curiosity made her pay attention to the details Camila often pointed out. Their visit had been equal parts work and wonder, though Valentina occasionally wished Camila's obsessive attention to detail didn't include losing track of time.

By the time they met up with Dae-hyun at a small tea shop, it was clear their self-proclaimed guide had more enthusiasm than knowledge.

"You said you knew the best spots for photos," Camila said, arching an eyebrow as she slid into a seat across from Valentina.

"I do!" Dae-hyun declared, dramatically pulling out a wrinkled map and spreading it over the table. "Bukchon is full of hidden gems—most guides won't even mention them."

Valentina studied the map skeptically. "Did you... mark all the convenience stores?"

"Those are snack stops," Dae-hyun explained, undeterred. "Essential for any to ur."

Camila sighed, but her lips twitched with amusement. "And here I thought you'd be leading us to historical treasures."

"Snacks are treasures," Dae-hyun countered, grinning.

The bell above the tea shop door jingled, and Joon-ho entered, looking both resigned and mildly curious. His gaze swept over the table, landing on the map, then shifted to Dae-hyun.

The next day unfolded with a steady rhythm of purpose. Joon-ho delivered the scroll to the museum, where he and Professor Im Hye-wonworked with the curator to carefully examine its intricate illustrations and faint text, confirming its connection to the staff and revealing hints of yet another artifact. Meanwhile, Dae-hyun entertained a group of tourists with his signature humor and theatrical storytelling, cleverly slipping in details about their adventure disguised as local legends. Camila and Valentina, stationed at a cozy café near the museum, outlined their article's structure, balancing historical depth with the allure of mystery. They coordinated with the museum's PR team to ensure accuracy and collaboration, cementing the day as a productive step toward unraveling the Path of Five Virtues.

Joon-ho and Dae-hyun met them at the café shortly after they were done. They came across Camila and Valentina speaking in hushed animated tones, in Spanish.

As they ordered tea and snacks, the conversation turned to language.

"So," Dae-hyun began, gesturing to Valentina, "why Spanish? Everyone here speaks English."

Valentina arched an eyebrow, her lips quirking into a smile. "Why not Spanish? It's my first language. And when you're in a country where you don't know the language, it feels... grounding. Less awkward."

Dae-hyun nodded thoughtfully. "Makes sense. It's like having a baby blankie."

Valentina arched her eyebrow. It was enough to make Dae-hyun cough and turn away.

He turned to Camila next. "And you? Why do you always speak Korean, even when English would be easier?"

Camila shrugged, her gaze drifting to the tea on the table. "Out of respect, mostly. I'm a guest here, so the least I can do is tr y. Even if I make mistakes, people usually appreciate the effor t."

"That's admirable," Joon-ho said quietly, his tone sincere.

Camila smiled. "It also helps with my work. I'm here to tell stories about Korea—its culture, history, people. I can't do that without understanding the language."

"Speaking of stories," Valentina said, her sharp editor's instincts kicking in, "what's your next one? That pottery shop you mentioned earlier?"

Camila nodded. "Yes. The owner's granddaughter told me about a family crest tied to a legend about virtues— empathy, resilience, and so on. It reminded me of something I read about the Path of Five Virtues."

Joon-ho froze for a fraction of a second, quickly masking his reaction with a sip of tea. "That's an old folktale," he said casually.

"Folktale or not," Camila pressed, "it keeps coming up. I feel like there's more to it."

Valentina grinned. "Sounds like Camila found your next lead Park ."

Dae-hyun, determined to bring attention back to himself, leaned forward dramatically. "And how lucky are you to have me as your guide? Without me, you'd still be wandering around snackless and clueless."

"Snackless, maybe," Camila said with a smirk. "But clueless? That's debatable."

Valentina chuckled. "I'd say our real luck is having a historian on board." She glanced at Joon-ho. "What do you think?"

Joon-ho hesitated, his guarded nature keeping him from fully engaging. "I think the more people involved, the more complicated things get."

"Complicated can be good," Valentina replied smoothly. "That's where the best stories come from."

As the group left the café, Camila slowed to take a photo of the street bathed in the warm glow of twilight. Joon-ho lingered nearby, his attention caught by the faded crest painted on a weathered hanok door.

As she turned to leave, Dae-hyun let out a low whistle. "Hyung, I like her. She's mysterious. The other one's scar y."

"She's a stranger," Joon-ho muttered, opening a weathered map with quick, precise movements.

"A stranger who knows a good story when she hears one," Dae-hyun countered, his grin undeterred.

Chapter 5: Even when the skies fall, I show you a way out; what am I?

"Back again?" the potter said, setting down his tools as Camila entered with the others in tow. His sharp eyes moved from her to Joon-ho, lingering for a moment. "And you've brought reinforcements."

"These are my colleagues," Camila said, gesturing to the group. "We're following up on what you shared about the phoenix and the Path of Five Vir tues."

The potter stood, brushing clay from his hands. His expression softened as he studied Joon-ho. "You're the historian, aren't you?"

Joon-ho inclined his head. "I am. And your pottery is known for its intricate symbolism. We're here to learn more."

The potter chuckled softly and bowed. "I am Um Soo-hyun. It's rare for anyone to come looking for meaning these days. Most people just want something pretty for their shelves." He gestured for them to sit near his wheel, where several pots with phoenix carvings were drying.

"These car vings," he began, pointing to the phoenix motifs, "are tied to the Path of Five Virtues. They represent rebirth, but more importantly, unity. The phoenix isn't just a symbol—it's a key to understanding how the virtues come together."

Camila leaned forward, taking notes as she listened. "And how do we use that key?"

The potter Um tilted his head, a faint smile on his face. "I've told you what I know, but if you're looking for answers, you need someone who seen more, deeper. There's a master woodcarver near the southern gate. He's worked on temple restorations across Korea and knows these symbols better than anyone."

"Do you know him personally?" Joon-ho asked, his curiosity piqued.

Um Soo-hyun nodded. "We've known each other some time. His name is Nam Joon-seok. He respects tradition and understands the importance of preserving stories. He'll recognize your sincerity—if you approach him with respect."

Dae-hyun, who had been inspecting a particularly elaborate vase, chimed in. "So, we're chasing carvings now? Sounds like fun. And maybe this guy has a good story or two."

Mr. Um smiled faintly, his eyes flicking to Dae-hyun. "He does, but don't mistake him for an entertainer. He values purpose over words. Remember that when you meet him."

With a respectful bow and the master potter's directions in hand, the group thanked him and left, the phoenix carvings etched in their minds as they made their way to the woodcarver's shop.

The narrow streets near the southern gate were lined with small shops and stalls selling everything from handcrafted jewelry to steaming dumplings. Camila led the group with purpose, their earlier visit to the pottery shop fueling her determination. The woodcarver's shop stood out immediately—a modest wooden building adorned with intricate carvings of cranes, lotus flowers, and a phoenix motif above the door.

"This is it," she said, reaching for the door to open for the others. Joon-ho smiled, then scowled at Dae-hyun who noticed.

"Some tour guide," he whispered to Dae-hyun. "Over-rated is more like it and you eat like an elephant."

Dae-hyun stuck out his tongue childishly as he raced to head the group and make a grandiose bow for them to enter the shop.

Inside, the smell of freshly cut wood filled the air. The walls were lined with panels depicting traditional Korean motifs, each more intricate than the last. At the center of the room stood a wiry man in his seventies, his hands steady as he worked on a small piece of sandalwood. He glanced up as they entered, his sharp eyes lingering on Camila.

The woodcarver's eyes shifted to Joon-ho, narrowing slightly. "You're the historian."

"First the potter, now the woodcarver. Two masters, completely unconnected, both knowing exactly who you are. Either Joon-ho's luck is unmatched, or something's guiding us into place."

Dae-hyun, leaning against the wall, straightened and looked at her with a half-smile. "Or maybe—just maybe—it's because Joon-ho actually deserves it. Then, with a small smirk, he added, "But sure, destiny works too, if it makes you feel better."

Joon-ho's gaze flicked to Dae-hyun briefly, his face unreadable. "Whatever it is, let's not get distracted. We're here for answers."

Valentina tilted her head, her smirk softening. "Fair enough. But you can't deny, it feels like the pieces are falling into place."

The woodcarver, overhearing, chuckled quietly. "Sometimes the path reveals itself when you stop looking for the why and start walking it."

The man's lips quirked in faint amusement. "You must know I don't speak lightly of legends. What you're chasing isn't just a story—it's a map, and I suspect you have the missing pieces."

Camila's brow furrowed. "How do you know we're looking for something? What do do you mean?"

The woodcarver took out his cellphone and laughed.

"I'm not a mind reader. Potter Um called to tell me to expect you and that you could be trusted."

He then got up and walked to a large panel leaning against the wall. He tilted it forward to reveal an intricate carving of a phoenix encircled by five symbols. "This is a replica of a map I once uncovered during a restoration at Haedong Yonggungsa Temple. The five symbols represent the Path of Five Virtues. But look here."

He pointed to two empty spaces within the phoenix's wings. "These gaps are meant to house objects—pieces that complete the map. Without them, the alignment is incomplete, and the path can't be fully understood."

Joon-ho stepped closer, pulling the scroll from his bag. "Mr. Nam, you're saying the staff and this scroll are the missing pieces?"

The master woodcarver nodded. "It's not coincidence you found them. The artifacts were scattered to protect the knowledge they hold. Together, they'll unlock the next step."

Valentina took notes furiously while Camila photographed the carving and the gaps. Dae-hyun, who had been quietly observing, finally spoke up. "So, we're not just chasing history—we're putting it back together."

The woodcarver smiled faintly. "Exactly. And with the pieces you've found, the map will finally begin to make sense."

Camila took photos and they thanked the master woodcarver for his time.

The group settled into a corner table at a bustling noodle shop near the southern gate. Bowls of steaming kalguksu arrived quickly, filling the air with the comforting aroma of garlic and broth. The table was soon cluttered with notebooks, maps, and Valentina's laptop as they debriefed.

"The map clearly shows five locations," Joon-ho said, gesturing to a sketch Camila had made from the woodcarver's panel. "But without the staff and scroll, we wouldn't have known how they align."

Camila nodded, flipping through her notes. "The staff and scroll aren't just artifacts—they're keys. And now we know where to look next."

Valentina sipped her tea thoughtfully. "This story keeps getting bigger."

Across the shop, a group of tourists laughed loudly, their voices cutting through the hum of conversation. Most of the group ignored them, but Dae-hyun's attention lingered on the man leading the table. He tilted his head slightly, squinting.

"Something wrong?" Camila asked, noticing his distraction.

Dae-hyun shrugged, a faint frown on his face. "That tour guide. I think I've seen him before. He used to run tours in this area, but he quit about a year ago. Left pretty suddenly, if I remember right."

"Is that unusual?" Valentina asked.

"Maybe," Dae-hyun replied, still watching the man. "He was good at his job— charming, popular. But there was always something... off about him. He doesn't belong with that group, though. They're tourists, but he looks like he's running a different kind of game."

Joon-ho glanced over briefly, his expression unreadable. "We should stay focused. If he's trouble, we'll deal with it if it comes to us."

Chapter 6: Mix me into myself, and you will find no change; what am I?

The early morning sunlight filtered through the curtains of Park Joon-ho's office where the group had gathered to finalize their day's plans. The scroll and the woodcarver's panel map, sketched out by Camila lay on the low table between them, alongside Valentina's detailed notes. Over steaming cups of barley tea, they reviewed their route to Namsan, where the next piece of the puzzle awaited them.

"The map is clear," Joon-ho said, his voice steady. "The symbols point to a specific shrine near the southern slope of the mountain. If the stories are true, the shrine hasn't been visited in decades—it's likely been forgotten by all but a f ew."

Valentina tapped her pen against her notebook. "And if it's forgotten, it means fewer prying eyes. That's good for us."

Camila adjusted her camera strap. "But also means we'll have to rely on what we've pieced together. No signs, no guides —just us and this map."

Dae-hyun leaned back in his chair, twirling his a rubber chicken in one hand. "Sounds like the perfect recipe for an adventure. I'll bring the comic relief, as always."

Joon-ho offered an annoyed sigh before standing. "We leave in an hour. Pack light —the terrain won't be forgiving. Leave the chicken. "

The trek to the base of Namsan was quieter than usual, the hum of Seoul fading as they entered the tree-lined trails. The path wound through the shadows of towering pines, their whispers carried by the cool breeze. The group's pace slowed as the terrain grew uneven, their destination—a forgotten shrine—beckoning with a quiet pull that none of them could explain.

Joon-ho led the way, his usual stoicism replaced with a subtle intensity. Camila noticed the shift and quickened her steps to walk beside him.

"You seem more invested than before," she said lightly, her gaze searching his face.

Joon-ho glanced at her, his expression serious but not dismissive. "It's not every day you stumble across something tied to both history and legend. I've spent my career studying artifacts that reveal how values shaped a society, but this..." He gestured vaguely to the path ahead. "This feels different."

"How so?"

Joon-ho hesitated before answering. "It's not just history—it's cultural identity. If the Path of Five Virtues was real, and if these artifacts exist, they weren't just symbols. They were a blueprint for how people lived and led."

Camila nodded thoughtfully. "And finding them would mean proving the values that bound a society together."

"Exactly," Joon-ho said, a flicker of admiration crossing his face.

The shrine appeared suddenly, nestled in a clearing where the trees parted to reveal a stone structure weathered by time. Its walls were adorned with faded carvings, the symbols faint but unmistakable: five distinct patterns, each representing one of the virtues.

"Wow," Valentina murmured, stepping closer. "This place looks like it's been forgotten for centuries."

Joon-ho's fingers brushed the carvings, his movements reverent. "These symbols... they're older than I expected. They predate most records of the Joseon Dynasty."

Dae-hyun crouched near the base of the shrine, picking up a loose stone. "So, what's the plan? Do we just... find the next artifact lying around?"

"It's not that simple," Joon-ho replied, his voice tinged with exasperation. "The artifacts were hidden intentionally. They weren't meant to be discovered by anyone who wasn't willing to understand their meaning."

"Sounds like a fancy way of saying we're on a scavenger hunt," Dae-hyun said, tossing the stone aside.

Camila smiled, her gaze sweeping over the carvings. "What do these mean, Joon-ho? The carvings, I mean."

Joon-ho traced one of the symbols with his finger. "They're representations of the virtues—empathy as an open hand, resilience as a rising sun, wisdom as an unfurling scroll, integrity as a straight line, and unity as a circle. Together, they form a map, but not one that's easy to read."

Valentina tilted her head. "A metaphorical map?"

"Exactly," Joon-ho said, his voice firm. "The path isn't just physical. It's about understanding and embodying these vir tues."

As the group explored the shrine, Camila noticed a faint indentation on one of the stone walls. She leaned closer, brushing away dirt to reveal a small, recessed compartment.

"Over here," she called, drawing the others' attention.

Joon-ho knelt beside her, carefully prying open the compartment. Inside was another weathered scroll, its edges frayed but its markings still legible.

He unrolled it slowly, his breath catching as he studied the contents. "It's another scroll. But this one's a map," he said softly.

Dae-hyun peered over his shoulder. "A real map this time? With X's and everything?"

Joon-ho ignored him, his focus unwavering. "This leads to the next location. It's farther south—Gyeongju, near the ancient capital of Silla."

Valentina crossed her arms. "So, we're heading deeper into history?"

Joon-ho nodded. "Silla was known for its philosophical advancements and emphasis on unity. It makes sense that one of the artifacts would be there."

As the group began their descent from the shrine, the mood shifted subtly. The discovery of the map had brought a renewed sense of purpose, binding them closer together.

Dae-hyun walked beside Valentina, his usual bravado softened. "So, what do you think of all this? Legends, artifacts, mystery?"

Valentina smirked. "It's intriguing. But I think you just like the idea of being part of a grand stor y."

Dae-hyun grinned. "Who wouldn't? You've got to admit, it's more fun with me around."

"You keep things... interesting," Valentina admitted grudgingly.

Camila, meanwhile, fell into step with Joon-ho. "You seem different," she observed.

Joon-ho glanced at her, his expression unreadable. "How so?"

"Less stiff. More willing to share," Camila said with a smile.

"Don't get used to it," Joon-ho replied, though his tone lacked its usual edge.

As they returned to the city, the group found themselves walking past a market alive with energy. Children laughed as they chased each other, vendors called out to passersby, and the scent of sizzling food filled the air.

Camila stopped to capture the scene, her camera clicking softly. " This," she said, "feels like unity."

Joon-ho paused beside her, his gaze distant. "It's the kind of unity the Path was meant to inspire. Not just harmony, but connection."

Dae-hyun, overhearing, nudged Joon-ho. "See? Even you can be poetic."

Joon-ho sighed but didn't respond, his thoughts clearly elsewhere.

Chapter 7: Speak my name, and you might see me appear; what am I?

The train to Gyeongju rattled through the countryside, leaving behind the towering skyscrapers of Seoul. Camila sat by the window, her camera poised, capturing fleeting glimpses of rolling green hills and rice paddies. Beside her, Valentina leaned back with her notebook, jotting down observations while occasionally side-eyeing Dae-hyun, who was quietly humming and fiddling with something in his bag.

Across the aisle, Joon-ho reviewed the scroll they had found, his brow furrowed in concentration. The soft murmurs of the group contrasted with the steady clatter of the train, each of them lost in their own thoughts—or, in Dae-hyun's case, schemes.

"Hyung," Dae-hyun said suddenly, breaking the silence. "Do you think the Silla Dynasty would've appreciated modern comedy?"

Joon-ho didn't even look up. "No."

"But think about it," Dae-hyun pressed. "What if I combined slapstick with historical anecdotes? 'Why did the Silla king cross the pond? To unify the provinces!'"

Valentina groaned. "Please tell me this is not your 'experimental phase.'"

Dae-hyun grinned. "Oh, you'll see. Great art takes risks."

Camila, fighting a smile, glanced at Joon-ho. "Is he always like this?"

"Worse," Joon-ho replied without missing a beat.

The ancient city welcomed them with a serene blend of history and modernity. The streets were quieter than Seoul's bustling avenues, lined with hanoks and quaint shops selling local delicacies and handicrafts.

"Welcome to the heart of the Silla Dynasty!" Dae-hyun announced grandly, spreading his arms as they stepped off the train. "Let me be your guide, your historian, and your comedian."

"More like our distraction," Valentina muttered, earning a chuckle from Camila.

Joon-ho, however, was already focused. "Wolji Pond is a short walk from here. It's the most likely place to find the next artifact."

Dae-hyun pretended to yawn. "Ah, yes. Another artifact. So thrilling. But first—" He pulled a map from his pocket and pointed to a street lined with food stalls. "—fuel for the journey."

Valentina glared. "Are you ever not thinking about food?"

"Actually, yes," Dae-hyun replied with mock seriousness. "I'm also thinking about timing. Comedy is all about timing."

With that cryptic comment, he began walking, the group reluctantly following.

The pond shimmered in the late afternoon light, its still surface mirroring the ruins of ancient pavilions. The air was heavy with history, each stone and weathered pillar a silent witness to centuries of culture and leadership.

"This place," Joon-ho began, his tone reverent, "was a symbol of unity during the Silla Dynasty. It's where leaders, philosophers, and artists gathered to shape the future of their kingdom."

"Sounds like a prime location for some light entertainment," Dae-hyun quipped, stepping onto a stone ledge.

Before anyone could stop him, he produced a rubber chicken from his bag and held it aloft like a sacred artifact.

"What the?! Didn't I tell you—" Joon-ho began, but Dae-hyun cut him off.

"Behold!" he said in a booming voice. "The chicken of wisdom! It sees all, knows all, and occasionally squeaks under pressure!"

To everyone's surprise, the absurdity of the moment broke the tension. Even Joon-ho let out an involuntary sigh, then chuckled as Dae-hyun squeezed the chicken, its high-pitched squeal echoing across the pond.

Camila, barely able to contain her laughter, snapped a photo. "You're ridiculous."

"Ridiculousness is an art form," Dae-hyun declared, bowing theatrically.

As the group explored the ruins, Camila noticed a faint carving on a fallen pillar near the water's edge. She knelt to examine it, brushing away dirt to reveal the familiar symbols: a circle surrounded by five smaller shapes.

"Over here," she called, motioning for the others.

Joon-ho crouched beside her, his expression intense. "This matches the carvings from the shrine," he said, tracing the lines with his finger. "The artifact must be nearby."

Valentina wandered toward a cluster of stones partially submerged in the pond. Something glinted beneath the water, catching the fading sunlight.

"Here," she said, pointing.

Joon-ho waded into the shallow water, carefully lifting a small golden seal from its resting place. The intricate design mirrored the circle symbol on the carvings.

"It's a royal seal," he said softly, holding it up for the group to see. "A symbol of unity used during the Silla Dynasty."

Camila snapped another photo, her voice tinged with awe. "This is incredible. It's not just an artifact—it's a piece of histor y."

As they dried off and gathered near the pond, Joon-ho studied the seal, his expression contemplative.

"The Path of Five Virtues wasn't just about moral guidance," he said. "It was a framework for governance, a way to ensure that leaders embodied these principles in every decision they made."

"And this seal represents unity," Camila added.

Joon-ho nodded. "Unity wasn't just about harmony. It was about creating connections—between people, ideas, and even across time."

Dae-hyun, still holding his rubber chicken, tapped it against the seal lightly. "So, we're basically rebuilding a legendary puzzle. And I'm here to keep morale high."

Valentina smirked. "By being ridiculous?"

"Exactly," Dae-hyun said, grinning.

As they began their walk back to the city, the air grew heavier, the weight of their discovery settling over them.

"Finding these artifacts feels like uncovering a secret someone didn't want found," Valentina said, her voice quiet.

Camila nodded. "It's not just about history. These were hidden for a reason."

"And what happens if someone less virtuous finds them?" Dae-hyun asked, his tone unusually serious.

Joon-ho's steps slowed, his gaze darkening. "That's what worries me."

The group fell silent, the distant lights of Gyeongju guiding them forward. For the first time, they felt the weight of the journey ahead—not just as an adventure, but as a responsibility

Chapter 8: From a humble stream, I rise to touch the skies; what am I?

The moon cast a silver glow over Gyeongju as the group retreated to their modest guesthouse for the night. The royal seal, now wrapped securely in a cloth pouch, sat on the table between them, radiating a quiet gravity. Each of them, in their own way, was captivated by the artifact's silent story, its connection to the Path of Five Virtues, and the promise of what lay ahead.

Joon-ho sat at the table, pouring over his notes with the seal resting beside him. The room was hushed except for the occasional scribble of his pen and Dae-hyun's subtle attempts to balance a spoon on his nose.

"Hyung," Dae-hyun finally said, breaking the silence. "Do you ever take a break? You've been staring at that thing for hours."

"This isn't a break kind of task," Joon-ho replied without looking up. "The markings on this seal align with inscriptions found in temple ruins throughout the Silla region. They're fragments of something larger."

Valentina, perched on the edge of the bed with her laptop, raised an eyebrow. "Larger how? Like another artifact?"

"Possibly," Joon-ho said. "But the inscriptions suggest more than physical artifacts. They point to a philosophy that shaped leadership and governance. The artifacts were meant to embody the virtues, but they were also meant to test those who sought them."

Camila leaned forward, her curiosity alight. " Test them how?"

Joon-ho hesitated, choosing his words carefully. "The artifacts aren't just hidden— they're protected. Their locations and the challenges surrounding them are meant to ensure that only those with true understanding and respect for the virtues can find them."

"Great," Dae-hyun said, tossing the spoon aside. "So we're not just looking for treasure; we're being judged by ancient ghosts."

"More like judged by ourselves," Camila said, her tone thoughtful.

Dae-hyun, sensing the mood growing too heavy, reached into his bag and produced the now-infamous rubber chicken.

"Perhaps," he said, squeezing the chicken for effect, "the next artifact will be hidden in plain sight, disguised as a humble fowl."

The squeak echoed through the room, earning a groan from Valentina and an exasperated look from Joon-ho.

"Why do you even carry that thing?" Valentina asked, pinching the bridge of her nose.

Dae-hyun grinned. "Because every great team needs comic relief. And you never know when a well-timed chicken can save the day."

Camila laughed, shaking her head. "You're unbelievable."

"And yet, indispensable," Dae-hyun replied with a mock bow.

As the laughter subsided, Camila turned to the group, her expression serious. "We need to decide how to move forward. Each artifact we find brings us closer to the heart of the Path of Five Virtues, but it also makes this more dangerous."

Valentina nodded. "If these artifacts were meant to guide leaders, they're not just historical relics. They're symbols of power. And symbols of power always attract the wrong kind of attention."

Joon-ho folded his notes, his expression unreadable. "The next step is to follow the inscriptions. They lead to another temple —this one deeper in the mountains near Andong. It's less well-known but historically significant."

"More hiking," Dae-hyun said with mock enthusiasm. "Wonderful."

Camila smirked. "I thought you liked adventure."

"I like adventures with snack breaks," Dae-hyun quipped. "And fewer hikes."

The group set out early the next morning, the royal seal carefully packed among their belongings. The train ride to Andong was quieter than the last, each of them preoccupied with their thoughts.

Valentina glanced at Joon-ho, who was absorbed in an old manuscript he had brought with him. "You've studied these artifacts before, haven't you?" she asked quietly.

Joon-ho hesitated before nodding. "I've come across references, but nothing concrete. This is the closest I've ever been to understanding their significance."

"Does it feel like we're getting closer?" Valentina pressed.

"Yes," Joon-ho said simply.

The trail to the temple was steep and overgrown, the air heavy with the scent of pine and moss. Dae-hyun's antics kept the group laughing despite the difficulty, his commentary ranging from exaggerated tales of his childhood to impromptu poetry inspired by their surroundings.

When they finally reached the temple, the sight took their breath away. Nestled among the trees, its weathered stones and intricate carvings seemed to hum with ancient energy.

Joon-ho approached the main gate, his movements reverent. "This is it," he said, his voice barely above a whisper. "The inscriptions match those on the seal."

As they entered the temple grounds, a faint carving on the floor caught Camila's eye. She knelt to examine it, brushing away the dirt to reveal another symbol of the virtues—this one depicting resilience.

"It's a clue," she said, motioning for the others.

Joon-ho studied the carving carefully. "It's more than that. It's a test."

"What kind of test?" Valentina asked warily.

"One that will require us to embody resilience," Joon-ho replied.

Dae-hyun grinned, holding up the rubber chicken. "Good thing I brought my secret weapon."

Chapter 9: I come unplanned, catching you unaware; what am I?

The air within the temple grounds felt heavier, as if the stones themselves carried the weight of centuries. The faint sound of rustling leaves accompanied the group's footsteps as they gathered around the newly uncovered carving. It depicted an intricate tree, its roots sprawling outward, interwoven with smaller symbols representing growth and endurance.

" This," Joon-ho said, gesturing to the carving, "is the marker of resilience. The tree symbolizes strength in adversity—how one grows despite challenges."

Valentina crossed her arms, her gaze sharp. "And how exactly do we prove we're resilient? Is there a secret handshake we're missing?"

"Not quite," Joon-ho replied, scanning the symbols. "These carvings are more than decorative—they're functional. They've always been designed to reveal the next step."

Dae-hyun crouched beside him, his grin playful. "And what if we can't figure it out? Do we just sit here until we sprout roots ourselves?"

Camila, who had been quietly studying the carving, pointed to a faint groove running along its edge. "Look at this. It's a channel —something's meant to flow through it."

As they examined the carving, Camila noticed a basin nearby, filled with rainwater. "Maybe the water activates it," she suggested.

Dae-hyun perked up. "Finally, something simple! I was expecting riddles or ghosts."

Valentina smirked. "Don't jinx it."

Joon-ho carefully filled a small cup with water and poured it into the groove. The liquid coursed along the intricate pathways of the carving, illuminating the tree's design with a faint golden glow.

The group watched in awe as the ground beneath the carving shifted, revealing a hidden passage leading down into darkness.

"Well, that's not ominous at all," Dae-hyun said, clutching his rubber chicken protectively.

Joon-ho stood, his expression resolute. "This is the trial. If we want to find the artifact, we'll have to go down there."

The passage was narrow and damp, the air thick with the scent of earth and stone. Camila led the way, her flashlight casting long shadows on the uneven walls.

"Remind me again why we're doing this," Valentina muttered, her voice echoing softly.

"Because history deserves to be uncovered," Camila replied, her tone light but determined.

"And because we're in too deep to back out now," Dae-hyun added cheerfully.

The tunnel opened into a small chamber, its walls covered in more carvings. At the center stood a pedestal holding a stone tablet etched with text.

Joon-ho stepped forward, his flashlight illuminating the inscription. "This is it," he murmured. "The test of resilience."

The inscription described a trial that required strength, patience, and trust. As Joon-ho read aloud, the chamber seemed to respond, the walls shifting to reveal three doors, each marked with a different symbol: a mountain, a river, and a flame.

"We have to choose," Joon-ho said, his brow furrowed. "Each door represents a different type of resilience—physical, emotional, or intellectual."

Camila glanced at the group. "Do we split up or stick together?"

" Together," Valentina said firmly. "Whatever's behind those doors, we're better off facing it as a team."

Dae-hyun held up the rubber chicken. "And with this, we're unstoppable."

Camila laughed despite herself. "Let's hope so."

They chose the door marked with the mountain, its symbolism of endurance resonating with the group. The passage beyond led to a cavern filled with jagged rocks and steep inclines. At the far end, a glowing artifact rested on a pedestal, its light casting eerie shadows.

As they navigated the treacherous terrain, the ground beneath them trembled. A section of the path collapsed, separating Camila and Joon-ho from Valentina and Dae-hyun.

"Stay where you are!" Joon-ho shouted. "We'll find another way across."

"Easy for you to say!" Dae-hyun called back, clutching Valentina's arm to steady her.

Camila glanced at Joon-ho. "We need to keep moving. They'll find their way."

Joon-ho nodded, his expression grim. "Resilience isn't just about surviving. It's about pushing forward, no matter the obstacles."

Camila and Joon-ho reached the pedestal first, the artifact glowing brightly—a small figurine of a tree, its branches entwined with gold. Joon-ho carefully lifted it, his reverence palpable.

"This represents growth through adversity," he said. "Resilience in its truest form."

Moments later, Valentina and Dae-hyun appeared, slightly dusty but unharmed.

" Told you we'd make it," Dae-hyun said, brushing dirt from his jacket. "No thanks to the crumbling floor."

Valentina smirked. "Your comedic timing almost got us killed."

"And yet, here we are," Dae-hyun said, holding up the rubber chicken triumphantly.

As they exited the cavern, the group felt a renewed sense of unity. The artifact now joined the royal seal in their collection, each piece bringing them closer to understanding the Path of Five Virtues.

"This is more than just a journey," Camila said quietly. "It's a reflection of what these virtues mean, and why they matter."

Joon-ho nodded. "And why they were hidden. These aren't just artifacts—they're lessons. And the deeper we go, the more we'll be tested."

Dae-hyun grinned. "Good thing we've got humor, brains, and good looks on our side."

Valentina rolled her eyes but smiled. "Let's just hope that's enough."

As the group made their way back to the surface, the sun breaking over the horizon, they couldn't shake the feeling that their journey was only beginning—and that the true test of resilience was yet to come.

Chapter 10: Alone I'm heavy, but with help, I'm light; what am I?

The sun dipped lower as the group left the Andong temple, their conversation subdued but their minds buzzing with questions. Joon-ho walked slightly ahead, his pace purposeful, his expression tighter than usual. He had been quiet since they uncovered the artifact of resilience, the weight of their discovery pressing heavily on him.

As they settled into a quiet guesthouse in Andong, the hum of cicadas outside the window a backdrop to the group's subdued conversations, Joon-ho sat at the small wooden desk in his room, a phone pressed to his ear. Across the room, Dae-hyun lounged on a futon, tossing the rubber chicken into the air absently.

"You're telling me you found what?" an excited and surprised voice coming from the phone.

Joon-ho sighed, his tone low. "It's a seal, sir. From the Silla Dynasty, tied directly to the Path of Five Virtues. We've also located a figurine symbolizing resilience. And that's why I called," Joon-ho interrupted. "I need guidance. We've uncovered something significant, but I can't risk the artifacts falling into the wrong hands."

Professor Choi's voice became serious instantly. "Bring them back to the museum. We'll create a plan to protect them. But be careful, Joon-ho. If word spreads, there will be consequences."

"I understand," Joon-ho said, hanging up. He turned to Dae-hyun, who had been quietly listening.

"Well?" Dae-hyun asked, catching the chicken mid-air.

"We take the artifacts to the museum," Joon-ho said firmly. "And no more detours. This isn't just about history anymore—it's about responsibility."

The next morning, Joon-ho gathered the group in his room. Camila and Valentina sat side by side, their expressions curious but cautious, while Dae-hyun leaned against the wall, still fiddling with the rubber chicken.

Joon-ho began. "It's been agreed. The artifacts need to be safeguarded at the museum. Once they're secure, we'll continue investigating the Path."

Camila frowned. "And what about us? We're part of this too."

"You are," Joon-ho said, his tone serious. "The museum has already recognized your contributions to this effort and have agreed to collaborate on your article. But I can't guarantee your safety. There are people—greedy people—who would do anything to take these artifacts. I need to know that you understand the risks."

Valentina crossed her arms. "We're not backing out. We knew this was more than just a story when you found the first artifact."

"Besides," Camila added, her tone softer, "we trust you, Joon-ho. You've been honest with us. And if the Path is about virtues, it's not just your responsibility—it's ours too."

Dae-hyun grinned. "And mine, of course." As if to not be forgotten, the rubber chicken squeaked in agreement.

As the group prepared to leave Andong, they stopped at a small café near the station. The atmosphere was cozy, with low wooden tables and the hum of conversation. It was there they were approached by an odd trio of foreigners, accompanied by a shifty-looking local guide. Strangely, the same group from that night at the noodle shop.

"Hi there," said the tallest of the three, a wiry man with an over-eager smile. "We couldn't help but notice you're into some serious adventuring the other night. Mind if we join you?"

Joon-ho glanced at Camila, his instincts instantly war y.

"I'm sorr y," Camila said politely, "but we're working on something private."

"Sure, sure, sure," the man said, pulling out his phone. "You know, our channel channel —'Treasures Unlocked.' We can feature you. Make you famous."

Valentina folded her arms. "No thanks. It's overrated."

"Oh, come on," the man said, flashing what he likely thought was a charming grin. "We've got a popular vlog —'Treasures Unlocked.' Ever heard of it?"

Valentina gave a tight smile. "Can't say that I have."

"It's huge!" chimed in one of the others, a man wearing a too-tight hiking outfit. "We'd love to feature you. You've got the look of a real stor y."

Dae-hyun tilted his head, eyeing the local guide, who was attempting to eavesdrop without subtlety. "Your guy looks like he belongs in a different kind of video. Aren't you Kim Sae-jin? Weren't you running tours to the zoo last year?"

The guide flushed a deep red and shook his head, but said nothing, fiddling with the straps of his worn-out backpack.

"Look ," the tall man pressed, "we're all treasure hunters here, right? Why not work together? Bigger team, bigger finds. It's a win-win."

Joon-ho's voice was icy. "We're not treasure hunters."

"No thanks," Joon-ho said firmly, standing.

The man's smile faltered, but he recovered quickly. "Sure, sure. It looks like a couple of matched sets. I get it. Not trying to block your love connections."

As the trio and their guide left, Dae-hyun squeezed the rubber chicken, its squeak breaking the tense silence.

"Was it just me," he said, "or did they scream, 'We're going to steal your stuff when you're not looking?'"

"Not just you," Valentina muttered.

Later, at the station, the group noticed the trio lingering near the platform, their eyes darting toward Joon-ho's bag. Even though the artifacts were safely at the museum, all of Joon-ho's notes and items were valuable and a lead towards more possible discoveries of artifacts.

Their instincts proved right later that evening when Joon-ho noticed one of the trio lurking near them yet again.

"They're watching us," he said quietly to Camila.

She glanced behind them, spotting the figure slipping into the shadows. "We need to move."

Joon-ho nodded. "The sooner we get back to the museum, the better."

At the station the group kept a low profile, their belongings packed securely. The train was already boarding when the trio and their guide appeared, trying—and failing—to act casual.

As they passed the group, the tall man gave a tight smile. "Safe travels."

Joon-ho didn't respond, his focus on getting everyone onto the train.

Dae-hyun, however, couldn't resist. "Don't lose your tour guide," he called, waving the rubber chicken. "He looks like he might wander of f."

"They're definitely up to something," Valentina muttered.

"I've got this," Dae-hyun said, stepping forward with his rubber chicken in hand.

"Dae-hyun, what are you doing?" Camila asked, alarmed.

"Being me," he said with a grin.

Walking directly toward the trio, Dae-hyun began an impromptu comedy act, complete with exaggerated bows and loud proclamations.

"Ladies and gentlemen! Welcome to today's exclusive performance: 'The Rubber Chicken Chronicles!'"

He squeezed the chicken, its squeak echoing across the platform. The treasure seekers froze, unsure whether to laugh or flee.

"This ancient artifact," Dae-hyun continued, holding up the chicken, "is said to bring fortune to the virtuous and confusion to the greedy. Care to test its powers?"

The trio exchanged uneasy glances, clearly uncomfortable with the attention they were drawing.

"Dae-hyun," Joon-ho called from behind, "we're boarding."

"Ah, duty calls!" Dae-hyun said, giving the chicken one last dramatic squeeze. "Farewell, friends! May your chickenless lives be fulfilling."

As he rejoined the group, Camila shook her head, laughing. "You're unbelievable."

"And yet, effective," Dae-hyun said, slipping the chicken back into his bag.

Once aboard the train, the group settled into their seats, the treasure seekers left behind on the platform.

Dae-hyun leaned back, his grin softer than usual. "You know, I don't just stick around for the laughs. I'd rather eat ramen in Seoul than let those guys get their hands on — my.. chicken." Dae-hyun had been looking at Valentina and suddenly felt flushed.

Valentina arched an eyebrow. "That's your way of saying you care?"

"Let's call it loyalty," Dae-hyun said, tossing the chicken into the air. "But don't tell anyone—I've got a reputation to maintain."

Camila stifled a laugh as they boarded and walked into the next car, leaving any thoughts of the trio behind.

Once the train was in motion, Joon-ho relaxed slightly.

"They'll keep trying to catch us with something," Valentina said. "People like that don't give up easily."

"They won't succeed," Joon-ho replied. "We're not doing this alone anymore. The museum will ensure any artifacts found will be protected."

Dae-hyun grinned. "And if they try again, I've got a secret weapon."

Camila laughed. "A neon pink secret weapon?"

"Never underestimate a trusted friend," Dae-hyun said with mock seriousness.

As the train carried them toward Seoul, the group shared a quiet moment of camaraderie.

Chapter 11: What's said in secret, I always know, whether sun shines or moonlight glows; what am I?

The morning sun cast a soft golden light over Jeonju's Confucian academy, the next place on the agenda, and the centuries-old buildings whispering of a time when scholars sought knowledge and enlightenment. The air was still, save for the rustling of leaves as the group stepped into the quiet grounds, following the clues left in the inscriptions.

Joon-ho led the way, his historian's instincts guiding them through the intricacies of the academy. The others followed, each contributing to the search in ways that would ultimately make the discovery of the artifact possible.

The academy grounds carried the weight of centuries, the crumbling stone paths and overgrown courtyards breathing quiet defiance against time. The team had spent hours deciphering carvings and piecing together symbols scattered across the grounds. Every discovery felt like a small triumph, each clue connecting with the next to form a fragile thread of meaning.

The group gathered near the central courtyard, where the afternoon sun cast long shadows across the uneven stones. Dae-hyun, leaning casually against a column, tapped his infamous rubber chicken against the ground absentmindedly. His gaze flicked between the carvings on the stones and the worn grooves etched into the nearby pillars.

"You know," he said, pointing to a small gap in the base of the column, "this feels like one of those moments where something clicks... or fits."

Joon-ho knelt to examine the space, running his fingers along the edges of the groove. "It's too precise to be random," he muttered. "This is part of the design. Something's supposed to go here."

Valentina crouched beside him, scanning the symbols on the pillar's surface. "It matches the alignment from the map," she said, gesturing toward the woodcarver's panel they had brought along. "This gap is intentional—but what fits into it?"

Camila knelt beside them, her brow furrowed as she studied the gap. "It's too small for the staff or the scroll. Whatever it is, it needs to be lightweight but precise."

Dae-hyun grinned, stepping forward and holding up his rubber chicken. "Well, this is lightweight, precise, and the perfect size. Call it destiny."

Valentina raised an eyebrow. "You can't be serious."

"Only one way to find out," Dae-hyun replied, carefully wedging the rubber chicken into the space. To everyone's surprise—and mild disbelief—it fit perfectly.

There was a soft click, followed by a low hum as the pillar shifted slightly. The grooves on the column lit up faintly, golden light tracing the carved patterns and connecting them to the stones beneath their feet.

"No way," Camila said, her voice filled with astonishment.

"Ridiculous genius," Dae-hyun corrected with a wink.

The light revealed a sprawling design etched into the courtyard, an intricate map that connected their previous discoveries —the staff, the scroll, and now the column. Joon-ho stood, his eyes tracing the glowing lines as they converged on a single point in the center of the courtyard.

"This is it," he said quietly. "The entire puzzle—it was all leading here."

Camila raised her camera, capturing the ethereal glow. "The center of the map. It's the final piece."

Dae-hyun stepped back, dusting off his hands. "Looks like my chicken saves the day again. I knew it was more than just a prop."

Valentina shook her head, half-amused, half-incredulous. "Of course it was the chicken. I should've known."

The group moved to the center, where a simple bronze plate was embedded in the ground, partially obscured by dirt and moss. Camila crouched down, brushing it clean to reveal more carvings that mirrored those on the staff and scroll.

Joon-ho knelt beside her, carefully lifting the plate. He turned it over in his hands, his expression both reverent and curious. "This plate connects everything. It completes the map. Look at what's underneath."

Valentina folded her arms, her gaze sharp. "But it's not just about the physical map, is it? It's about what it represents. The Path of Five Virtues—it's a legacy, not a treasure."

Camila nodded, her voice thoughtful. "The staff, the scroll, this plate—they were hidden to protect the virtues, not hoard them. It's about preserving what they stand fo r."

Joon-ho trembled slightly as he lifted the plate. Hidden under the plate, in the dirt, revealed a cloth wrapped in fabric strings. He gingerly dusted it off and opened it to reveal a jade figurine shaped like an open book.

Joon-ho carefully lifted it, his voice filled with awe. "The artifact of wisdom. It represents understanding as the foundation of leadership and learning."

As the group emerged from the grounds, their relief was short-lived. The unsavory trio and their shifty guide were waiting at the far end of the courtyard, their expressions a mix of frustration and suspicion.

"Well, well," the tallest man said, his tone forced. "Fancy meeting you here."

Camila's hand instinctively went to her bag. "We don't have time for this," she muttered.

"Relax," Dae-hyun said, stepping forward with the rubber chicken. "They're just here for the show."

He squeezed the chicken dramatically, its squeak echoing across the courtyard. The trio hesitated, their confidence wavering.

"Let's go," Joon-ho whispered.

The group moved quickly, weaving through the academy grounds and slipping into the busy streets of Jeonju's hanok village.

By the time they reached the home of Mrs. Tae Ji-yoon, the local historian, the sun was setting. The jade figurine was placed in her care. She would take the artifact to the museum.

"You've done well," Mrs. Ta said, her voice calm. "But your journey isn't over. The Path will continue to test you."

"There's more? Well, we're ready?" Camila said, her tone resolute.

Dae-hyun grinned. "And if we're not, I've got a chicken for backup."

Valentina groaned, but there was a fondness in her expression. "You're impossible."

"And yet, indispensable," Dae-hyun replied.

That evening, over tea at a small inn, the group reflected on their experience.

"These artifacts were hidden for a reason," Joon-ho said. "Not just to preserve history, but to remind us of the values that shaped it."

"And it's those values that helped us find them," Camila added.

Valentina nodded. "We couldn't have done this alone."

Dae-hyun leaned back, his grin softening. "We make a pretty good team, don't we?"

Camila and Valentina nodded silently, unaware that Joon-ho had joined them.

Chapter 12: With patience and persistence, even the strongest will yield; what am I?

The quiet of Hahoe Village gave the impression of safety, but the group was learning not to trust appearances. Each artifact they uncovered drew more attention, and the unsavory trio lurking in their shadows made every step feel precarious. As they reached the outskirts of the village, the massive zelkova tree that Joon-ho had identified came into view, its twisted branches stretching skyward like an ancient sentinel.

"This has to be it," Joon-ho said, his pace quickening.

Valentina followed, scanning their surroundings with sharp eyes. "Let's make this fast. I don't like how exposed we are here."

The tree stood tall and imposing, its base gnarled and worn by time. Camila knelt to examine the carvings on its trunk, brushing away dirt and moss to reveal faint markings.

"These match the ones we saw in Jeonju," she said, pointing to a series of intricate symbols etched into the bark. "It's definitely connected to the artifact."

Joon-ho joined her, running his fingers over the carvings. "It's a map," he murmured. "But it's encoded—there's a pattern here that we need to decipher."

"Great," Valentina said, crossing her arms. "Another puzzle."

"Not just a puzzle," Joon-ho corrected. "This is a test. The artifact of integrity wouldn't be left unguarded. It's hidden in a way that ensures only those with the right values can find it."

The group spread out around the tree, each contributing to uncovering the artifact's location.

Camila used her camera to capture close-ups of the carvings, zooming in on faint details that were otherwise invisible to the naked eye. "These lines—they form a sequence," she said, pointing to the images on her screen.

Valentina followed the sequence, her analytical mind piecing together the logic behind the symbols. "It's a code," she said. "Each carving corresponds to a step in the process. We need to activate something."

Joon-ho provided historical context, recognizing a phrase embedded in the symbols: " Trust in the unseen." He explained that this was a key Confucian principle tied to integrity. "It means relying on values and intuition, even when the path isn't clear," he said.

Dae-hyun, uncharacteristically serious, used his quick reflexes to uncover a hidden lever concealed among the roots. "It was right here all along," he said, stepping back to let Joon-ho inspect it.

When the lever was pulled, the ground beneath the tree shifted, revealing a small stone compartment. Inside was a bronze medallion engraved with the word "Integrity" in Hangul, its surface polished to a gleaming finish despite centuries in hiding.

Joon-ho lifted it carefully, his voice filled with awe. "The artifact of integrity. It represents trust, the cornerstone of leadership."

Before the group could celebrate, the sound of hurried footsteps reached their ears. Turning, they saw the treasure seekers and their guide emerging from the nearby path, their expressions a mix of irritation and determination.

"Well, look at that," the tall man said, his voice dripping with forced charm. "You've gone and found something special. Care to share?"

Camila instinctively stepped closer to Joon-ho, shielding the artifact with her body. "We're not interested in whatever deal you're trying to make."

The man's smile faltered, and he nodded to his companions. "Plan B, then."

As the trio advanced, Dae-hyun stepped forward, brandishing his rubber chicken. "Alright, folks! Time for the grand finale!"

But this time, the treasure seekers were ready. The guide lunged forward, snatching the chicken from Dae-hyun's hand and tossing it aside.

"Hey!" Dae-hyun shouted, his face a mix of shock and outrage. "That was a collector's item!"

With Dae-hyun momentarily disarmed, Valentina stepped into the fray. Switching to Spanish, she raised her voice, calling out loudly to draw attention from nearby tourists.

"¡Ayuda! ¡Ven a ver esto!" she shouted, gesturing wildly toward the trio. "¡Estas personas están actuando de forma sospechosa!"

Her dramatic tone and commanding presence worked perfectly. Curious tourists began to gather, murmuring among themselves as they watched the scene unfold.

The tallest treasure seeker hesitated, clearly uncomfortable under the growing scrutiny. "What's she saying?" he muttered to his companions.

"Nothing good," the woman replied, glancing nervously at the onlookers.

While Valentina kept the crowd engaged, Camila used her camera to take close-up shots of each treasure seeker, making a point of snapping their faces from multiple angles.

"Smile for the camera," she said sweetly, clicking the shutter. "Your faces are going viral."

The treasure seekers froze, their unease palpable.

"Delete those," the tall man demanded, his voice low.

"Not a chance," Camila replied, her tone icy.

With the growing crowd and the mounting pressure of Camila's camera, the treasure seekers began to retreat. "This isn't over," the tall man hissed as they backed away.

"Yeah, yeah," Dae-hyun said, waving them off. "Don't forget to subscribe to our channel for more misadventures."

Once the trio disappeared, the group wasted no time. They secured the artifact in Joon-ho's bag and hurried toward the village's main road.

By the time they reached Mrs. Tae's home, the tension had begun to ease. The guardian accepted the artifact with quiet reverence, her calm presence a stark contrast to the chaos they had just escaped.

"You've done well," she said, placing the medallion alongside the others.

Camila sighed, sinking into a nearby chair. "It's getting harder to stay ahead of them."

"But we're getting better at it," Valentina said with a small smile.

Dae-hyun, still rubbing his hands where his chicken had been taken, smirked. "Next time, I'm bringing a backup chicken."

Joon-ho shook his head, but there was a hint of a smile on his face. "Let's just focus on what's next."

That evening, over tea, the group reflected on the journey so far.

"These artifacts are more than histor y," Joon-ho said. "They're tests of who we are and what we value."

"And they're showing us how we work together," Camila added.

Valentina nodded. "We couldn't have done this alone."

Dae-hyun leaned back, his grin softening. "It's teamwork, folks. And a little luck ."

Chapter 13: The longer the road, the more tales I hold; what am I?

The next leg of the journey brought the group to Boseong, known for its sprawling green tea fields and tranquil landscapes. The inscriptions Joon-ho had deciphered from the previous artifact pointed to this area, suggesting that the artifact of empathy was tied to the lives of those who worked the land—a virtue built on understanding and shared human experiences.

The group arrived at a quaint inn nestled on the edge of the fields, its wooden beams and thatched roof blending seamlessly with the surrounding greenery. The innkeeper, a cheerful elderly woman, welcomed them warmly.

"Your timing is perfect," she said. " Tonight is the village's Moonlight Festival. You must join us. It's a celebration of unity and gratitude."

Joon-ho exchanged a glance with the others. "A festival might be the perfect way to learn more about the artifact's location."

"And blend in," Valentina added. "We don't need anyone else finding us before we find it."

Dae-hyun grinned. "Festival means food. I'm in."

The festival was a lively affair, with lanterns illuminating the tea fields and music filling the air. Villagers gathered to share stories, dance, and enjoy an array of traditional dishes.

Camila wandered through the crowd, her camera capturing the vibrant atmosphere. She paused near a group of farmers, their laughter and camaraderie infectious.

"This is what empathy looks like," she thought, watching as they shared stories of their struggles and triumphs.

Meanwhile, Valentina joined a group of women weaving flower crowns, her curiosity drawing her into their circle. Though her Korean was limited, her genuine interest bridged the gap, and soon she was laughing along with them.

Dae-hyun, of course, found himself at the center of attention, entertaining a group of children with his slapstick antics. His comedic timing brought smiles to their faces, their laughter ringing through the night.

Joon-ho, ever the scholar, quietly observed from the edges of the festival. He noticed an older man sitting alone near a small shrine, his expression thoughtful.

Approaching the man, Joon-ho bowed respectfully. "Excuse me, sir. May I sit with you?"

The man gestured for him to join. "You're not from here," he said.

"No, but we're trying to understand the history of this place," Joon-ho replied. "I've heard there's a story tied to this shrine."

The man nodded, his eyes distant. "The shrine honors those who worked these fields long before us. It's said that an artifact was left here as a reminder of the importance of understanding and compassion for one another. But it's been lost for generations."

"Do you believe it still exists?" Joon-ho asked.

The man smiled faintly. "If you look with the right eyes and the right heart, you might find it."

The group reconvened later that night at the shrine. The moonlight bathed the small stone structure in a soft glow, and the air was filled with the faint scent of tea leaves.

"This is it," Joon-ho said. "The artifact is here—it has to be."

"But where?" Valentina asked, scanning the area.

Camila crouched near the base of the shrine, her fingers brushing against the weathered stone. "There's something carved here," she said, pointing to faint symbols.

Joon-ho knelt beside her, his eyes narrowing. "These are similar to the carvings we've seen before."

The carvings led them to a nearby tea field, where rows of neatly trimmed bushes stretched into the distance. Among the plants, they discovered a series of small, hidden markers—symbols etched into the earth itself.

"This is a trail," Joon-ho said, his excitement growing. "We need to follow it."

As they moved through the field, the group began to understand the significance of the trail. Each marker told a story of those who had worked the land— of sacrifices made, struggles endured, and victories celebrated.

Camila used her camera to document the markers, preserving the stories they uncovered.

Valentina analyzed the patterns, piecing together the narrative behind the symbols.

Joon-ho provided context, drawing on his knowledge of local history to connect the markers to the lives they represented.

Dae-hyun, surprisingly, offered moments of levity and insight, his humor lightening the mood while his observations added depth to their understanding.

The trail ended at an old tree at the edge of the field, its roots sprawling outward like open arms. Beneath one of the larger roots, they found a small stone box. Inside was a delicate porcelain figure of a hand, its palm open.

Joon-ho carefully lifted it, his voice filled with awe. "The artifact of empathy. It represents the power of understanding and shared humanity."

Camila smiled, her camera capturing the moment. "This one feels different. More personal."

As the group began to leave, the familiar voices of the treasure seekers echoed through the field.

"Well, isn't this a cozy scene," the tall man said, stepping into view.

"Don't you all have other people to stalk? Should I just dial 1-1-9 now?!"

Camila immediately began taking photos of the trio, her lens zooming in on their faces.

"Seriously?" the man muttered, trying to shield his face.

"Your faces will look great online," she said sweetly. "You're going to be famous for all the wrong reasons."

Valentina stepped forward, switching to Spanish. "¡Ladrones ineptos! ¡Todos los van a conocer!"

The man hesitated, clearly unnerved by the growing attention. "Let's go," he said to his companions. "This isn't over."

As they retreated, Dae-hyun smirked. "They keep saying that, but it feels pretty over to me."

Later that evening, the group entrusted the artifact to Professor Im Hye-won who lived nearby.

"You've done well," Yoon said, bowing deeply. "The virtue of empathy is safe once more."

As they left the village, the group felt a renewed sense of purpose. The Path of Five Virtues was nearing its final destination, they could feel it.

Chapter 14: Hear me a hundred times, but see me once to truly know; what am I?

The group arrived in Seoul with a mixture of relief and apprehension. The journey so far had been physically demanding, emotionally charged, and intellectually challenging, but it had also strengthened their bond. Each artifact they secured seemed to deepen their understanding of the Path of Five Virtues—and of each other.

Joon-ho led them to another quiet café near the National Museum, where they planned to regroup before seeking guidance from Professor Choi. The last inscriptions hinted at the final artifact, unity, but they were vague. It was clear, however, that the stakes were higher than ever.

As they sipped their tea, Valentina noticed a familiar figure loitering across the street.

"The tall one's back," she said, nodding subtly toward the treasure seeker from Boseong.

Dae-hyun turned in his seat, his smile fading. "And he's not alone. Look."

Two of his companions and their shifty guide joined him, their hushed conversation and darting glances suggesting they were planning their next move.

"We can't let them follow us to the museum," Joon-ho said. "If they think we've found something, it'll put everyone at risk."

"We need to lose them," Camila said, her tone firm. "But how?"

The group devised a plan to split up and confuse their pursuers.

Camila and Valentina would take the subway to a crowded market, drawing attention with Camila's camera while blending into the bustling crowds.

Joon-ho and Dae-hyun would head toward the museum, taking a roundabout route through quieter streets to avoid being followed.

"We'll meet back at the museum in two hours," Joon-ho said. "Be careful."

The market was alive with color and sound, a sensory overload of sights, smells, and activity. Camila snapped photos of street vendors and performers, her presence drawing attention from locals and tourists alike.

Valentina leaned in, speaking in Spanish to Camila while gesturing animatedly. "Let's make it look like we're the ones with the artifacts. They're watching."

Camila nodded, slipping a small pouch into her bag in a way that appeared deliberate. The treasure seekers, trailing at a distance, exchanged excited whispers.

"Think they're buying it?" Camila asked, her voice low.

"They're practically salivating," Valentina replied, smirking.

Meanwhile, Joon-ho and Dae-hyun moved swiftly through Seoul's quieter alleys, their pace brisk but unhurried.

"You think they'll catch on?" Dae-hyun asked, glancing over his shoulder.

"Not if we stay ahead of them," Joon-ho replied. "They're desperate, which makes them reckless."

Dae-hyun grinned. "Good thing we've got brains and comedy on our side."

As they approached the museum, Dae-hyun suddenly grabbed Joon-ho's arm. "Wait."

"What is it?"

Dae-hyun pointed to a reflection in a shop window. "One of them's tailing us. Looks like the guide."

Joon-ho sighed. "We'll need a distraction."

Dae-hyun darted into a nearby convenience store, emerging moments later with a large bag of snacks.

"Seriously?" Joon-ho asked, exasperated.

" Trust me," Dae-hyun said, tossing a handful of chips into the air as they walked.

The guide hesitated, clearly torn between following them and avoiding the attention Dae-hyun's antics were drawing. A few curious passersby even stopped to watch, laughing as Dae-hyun balanced a snack bag on his head while walking backward.

By the time they reached the museum's side entrance, the guide was gone.

"Never doubt the power of snacks," Dae-hyun said with a triumphant grin.

Camila and Valentina arrived shortly after, their expressions victorious.

"They took the bait," Valentina said. "Last we saw, they were searching every stall in the market."

Professor Choi greeted them inside, his expression grave. "You've done well to avoid them, but they're getting bolder. The next artifact is the most important—it represents unity, the cornerstone of the Path. If they get to it first..."

"They won't," Joon-ho interrupted. "Where do we start?"

Professor Choi unfurled a map of Korea, pointing to the coastal city of Busan.

"According to the inscriptions, the artifact of unity is tied to a temple overlooking the sea," he said. "It's a place where people have gathered for centuries to find peace and connection. But the exact location isn't clear. You'll need to search carefully."

Dae-hyun raised an eyebrow. "Busan? Sounds like a good place for a grand finale."

"Let's hope it's not too grand," Valentina muttered.

As the group prepared to leave for Busan, the weight of the journey ahead settled over them. Each artifact had brought them closer to the heart of the Path of Five Virtues, but it had also tested them in ways they hadn't anticipated.

"This one's going to be different," Joon-ho said quietly as they boarded the train.

Camila glanced at him. "How so?"

"Unity isn't just about finding an ar tifact," he replied. "It's about proving we can truly work as one."

Dae-hyun leaned back in his seat, the rubber chicken newly replaced. "Well, if anyone can do it, it's us."

Valentina smirked. "Let's hope you're right."

As the train pulled out of the station, the group felt a mixture of anticipation and resolve.

The Guardians of the Path

There's a quiet story whispered among those who know to listen—a tale of five who, long ago, took it upon themselves to protect the legacy of the Path of Five Virtues. They had never seen the artifacts themselves, only studied the symbols, the myths, and the meaning behind them. Yet they understood their importance better than anyone else.

It wasn't a mission assigned to them; no king or council had charged them with this role. It was a purpose they chose, bound by an unspoken pact. They knew the artifacts were never meant to be possessed, only preserved for those who could embody the virtues they represented. And so, they became silent sentinels, each guarding their piece of history in plain sight—watching, waiting, testing.

For decades, their work was a shadow in the corner of Korea's historical narrative. Each carried the weight of this duty quietly, their lives dedicated not to seeking the artifacts, but ensuring they would never be misused. They kept the greedy at bay and observed the good-hearted from a distance, always waiting for someone worthy to find their way.

When the staff was discovered, it was the Guardians of the Path who approached the curator, revealing the guardians' purpose. The curator, astonished and sworn to secrecy, realized he was now part of a story much larger than himself—a story guided not by power, but by trust and quiet vigilance.

And so, the memory of the guardians lingers, not in grand museums or official records, but in the quiet moments of those who dared to seek the Path and found wisdom waiting instead of treasure.

Chapter 15: No matter the struggle, my good end will make all worthwhile; what am I?

The train ride to Busan was quieter than the group expected. They had reached the final stage of the Path of Five Virtues, with only the artifact of unity left to uncover. The subtle tension hung in the air, not just from the weight of their mission, but from the ever-looming threat of the treasure seekers.

"The artifact of unity," Joon-ho said, staring at his notebook. "It's the most elusive one. The inscriptions don't give any clear directions—just references to trust, harmony, and connection. This won't be straightforward."

"Nothing has been," Valentina said, leaning back in her seat. "But we've figured everything out so far. We'll figure this out too."

Dae-hyun popped a piece of dried squid into his mouth. "And if we don't, at least we'll be in Busan. Great seafood."

The group arrived at Haedong Yonggungsa as the late afternoon sun bathed the coastline in a golden glow. The temple's ancient architecture stood resolute against the backdrop of crashing waves, its grounds bustling with visitors.

The temple was quiet, its weathered façade blending into the forest as though it had grown there over centuries. The group approached with purpose, their steps slowing instinctively as the ancient structure seemed to exude a calm authority. The courtyard stretched before them, bordered by stone walls etched with faded symbols, their meanings long forgotten by most.

"Unity," Joon-ho said, his voice low as they reached the threshold. "This place has always been about bringing people together. If the artifact is here, it won't just be hidden—it will require us to work as one."

The group spread out across the temple grounds, each drawn to different areas by their own instincts. Camila lingered near a low stone table beneath the gnarled branches of an ancient tree. Valentina was drawn to a cluster of prayer stones stacked in uneven piles. Joon-ho paced the perimeter, his gaze sharp, while Dae-hyun, ever restless, wandered toward the main hall.

Camila knelt by the stone table, brushing away a layer of dirt and leaves. The surface revealed faint, circular grooves, each about the size of a small bowl. "These aren't natural," she said, tilting her head. "It's like... they're meant to hold something."

Meanwhile, Valentina ran her fingers over the prayer stones, noticing a few were heavier than they looked. "These feel... weighted," she said aloud, lifting one and shaking it gently. Something rattled inside.

Joon-ho joined her, taking the stone and examining it closely. "It's hollow," he confirmed, finding a seam along its edge. With a careful twist, the stone came apart, revealing a small ceramic orb inside.

Across the courtyard, Dae-hyun's voice rang out. "Uh, guys? You're gonna want to see this."

The group followed his call to the main hall, where he stood in front of an ornate altar. The structure, though worn, bore an unmistakable pattern—a series of shallow depressions arranged in a circular design. "I'm no historian," Dae-hyun said, "but this thing is screaming 'puzzle.'"

Joon-ho studied the altar, then turned back to Camila. "The grooves on the stone table," he said, glancing at the ceramic orb in his hand. "And these depressions—this is all connected. We need to find more of these."

The search became a dance of individual strengths. Camila's sharp eye for detail led her to discover another hollow prayer stone hidden among the stacks. Valentina's analytical mind pieced together a pattern in the carvings on the temple walls, guiding them to yet another orb embedded in a crevice. Dae-hyun, with his unpredictable ingenuity, used his rubber chicken to nudge loose an orb lodged high in the branches of a tree, earning an incredulous laugh from Camila.

When they returned to the altar, they had five ceramic orbs, each etched with faint symbols. "Five orbs," Joon-ho said, carefully placing them into the circular depressions on the altar. "This must be the final step."

As they placed the orbs, the group noticed they each needed to rotate simultaneously. Without a word, they took positions around the altar, each gripping an orb. The silence was electric as they began to turn them in unison. At first, the movements were uneven, the orbs resisting their efforts.

"Steady," Joon-ho said, his voice calm but firm. "It has to be together."

Valentina adjusted her grip, her movements aligning with Joon-ho's. Camila matched their rhythm, her focus sharp. Dae-hyun, grinning despite the tension, added a deliberate twist.

With a final, synchronized turn, a soft chime resonated through the courtyard. The altar 's center shifted, revealing a hidden compartment. Inside lay a bronze medallion, its surface engraved with a simple design of interwoven threads.

Joon-ho lifted it reverently, his voice quiet. "Unity. Not just in name, but in action."

The group exchanged glances, the weight of the moment sinking in. This wasn't just a test of skill—it was a testament to their journey, one that demanded their unique strengths to uncover something far greater than themselves. And as the temple seemed to settle back into its timeless stillness, they knew they had become part of a story that would echo long after they were gone.

As they emerged from the pavilion, their triumph was interrupted by the familiar sound of hurried footsteps. The treasure seekers and their guide appeared, their expressions a mixture of frustration and desperation.

"Don't even think about it," the tall man said, stepping forward. "That artifact belongs to us."

"It belongs to history," Joon-ho replied calmly.

The shifty guide, emboldened, stepped closer. "Hand it over. Now."

Valentina stepped in front of Joon-ho, her voice sharp. "Get lost. You've done nothing but disrespect these places and the people who care for them."

Camila, meanwhile, began snapping photos of the group, her camera clicking rapidly. "Smile," she said coldly. "Your faces are about to be very well-known."

The treasure seekers hesitated, their confidence faltering.

"This isn't over," the tall man said, his voice low. He started to move forward towards them, the other two ready to follow his lead.

The scene unfolded in chaos. Dae-hyun was busy distracting them with his antics, while Joon-ho maintained his calm exterior as if anticipating a reprieve from these people. Camila and Valentina exchanged puzzled glances, wondering how this standoff would end.

A faint roar echoed in the distance. Heads turned as the sound grew louder—a deep, resonating hum of a powerful motorcycle. The treasure seekers stopped mid-argument, and even Dae-hyun paused, his rubber chicken dangling uselessly in his hand.

The motorcycle slid to a halt with impressive precision, the rider kicking up a small cloud of dust. He dismounted in one fluid motion, removing his sleek helmet to reveal a chiseled jawline and perfectly styled hair that could rival any K-pop idol. Dressed in a leather jacket with "Interpol" subtly stitched on the shoulder, Inspector Wong surveyed the scene, his piercing gaze taking in everything with a calm authority. From the shadows emerged two local police officers, who efficiently cuffed the group.

Camila blinked, momentarily at a loss for words. "Is he... real?" she whispered to Valentina.

Valentina, for once, was speechless.

Joon-ho stepped forward, trying to suppress a smirk. " Took you long enough, Jiaqi."

Inspector Wong's expression softened slightly. " Traffic," he replied, his voice smooth and commanding. "Hyung, even motorcycles can't outrun Seoul's gridlock."

Dae-hyun's jaw dropped as recognition dawned. "Wong? Jiaqi?" His surprise quickly turned to alarm. "Wait... is she still mad at me?"

Inspector Wong's calm demeanor faltered as he sighed. "Mad? Try livid. Jen still brings up the time you convinced her I was needed as a "security consultant" for a "new immersive tour ". "She eventually realized 'the tour' was just a brewery visit designed to sneak me out to go drinking. She wasn't happy man. I paid for that for weeks!"

Camila and Valentina exchanged looks, the tension breaking as they tried to stifle their laughter.

Inspector Wong turned to the treasure seekers, who were now frozen in place and in cuffs.

"Interpol has been tracking your activities for months," he said, his voice sharp and authoritative. "You've been stealing artifacts across Asia, and now, your little bogus channel escapade in Korea ends here."

The treasure seekers stammered, trying to backpedal. "We were just tourists—"

Dae-hyun interrupted, holding up the rubber chicken like a badge of authority. "Oh sure, vloggers with counterfeit maps and picklocks. Ver y believable."

Before the treasure seekers could respond, Wong snapped his fingers and the officers began leading them away.

One of the treasure seekers turned back, shouting, "You haven't seen the last of us!"

Dae-hyun, ever quick with a comeback, waved the rubber chicken dramatically. "Yeah, yeah, say hi to your cellmates for me!"

Inspector Wong removed his helmet in one smooth motion, revealing his flawlessly styled hair and ruggedly athletic features. His intense gaze swept across the group, lingering for a moment on Camila and Valentina.

With a charming smile that could melt glaciers, he extended a hand toward the women, first to Camila. "Inspector Wong," he said, his voice smooth as silk. "Interpol. I hope these fools didn't cause you too much trouble."

Camila blinked, then placed her hand in his, her cheeks flushing slightly. "I—uh—they—" she stammered, for once at a loss for words.

Turning to Valentina, Wong's smile widened ever so slightly, as if he knew his effect. "You must be part of this impressive team. I've heard great things."

Valentina, typically composed, muttered something unintelligible in Spanish. Camila elbowed her, and they exchanged a look that screamed, Is this man even real?

Joon-ho cleared his throat loudly, stepping between them. "Alright, Jiaqi, no need to overdo it."

Dae-hyun snorted. "Yeah, stop making us look bad. Some of us don't have K-drama hair."

Inspector Wong glanced at them, an almost imperceptible smirk on his face. "Jealousy doesn't suit you, Dae-hyun."

Inspector Wong's expression softened as he addressed the group. "Are you all alright? No injuries?" His concern was genuine, his tone sincere.

"We're fine," Joon-ho replied curtly, his arms crossed. "Though the rubber chicken nearly caused collateral damage."

Wong raised an eyebrow at the mention of the chicken but wisely chose to let it slide.

Turning back to Dae-hyun and Joon-ho, Wong's tone shifted, a conspiratorial glint in his eye. "By the way, it's been too long. We should sneak out for drinks soon— maybe hit the sauna after."

Dae-hyun's face lit up. "Now you're talking! The old gang back together again!"

Wong's smile faded slightly as he turned to Dae-hyun, his voice dropping into a mock-warning tone. "But Dae-hyun, I'm serious. If you don't grow up, my wife will make sure you regret it. She's still planning revenge for that night you convinced her to let me out."

Joon-ho smirked. "She doesn't forget, does she?"

"Not a chance," Wong replied with a chuckle. "And Dae-hyun, if you show up with that rubber chicken, you're on your own."

Wong turned back to Camila and Valentina, giving them each a respectful nod. "Ladies, it's been a pleasure. I hope the rest of your journey is less chaotic. Though with these two," he gestured to Joon-ho and Dae-hyun, "I wouldn't count on it."

Inspector Wong smirked as he donned his helmet. "Don't worry, Dae-hyun. Jen's too busy planning how to make you apologize properly. I'd start practicing groveling if I were you."

As he mounted his motorcycle, the women watched in awe, Camila biting her lip to suppress a grin. The engine roared to life, and Wong glanced back once more. "Try to stay out of trouble," he called, his smirk dazzling, before speeding off into the distance.

With that, Wong revved his motorcycle, the engine growling as he sped off into the distance, leaving everyone staring after him.

Dae-hyun sighed dramatically. "Why does he get the motorcycle, the authority, and the perfect hair? Life is unfair."

Valentina smirked. "Maybe because he doesn't carry around a rubber chicken."

Camila burst out laughing as Joon-ho finally cracked a small smile.

"Perfectly annoying," Dae-hyun muttered, holding up the rubber chicken. "But I'm keeping this. It's my trademark now."

"What movie did he walk out of?" Camila asked Joon-ho, her tone layered with curiosity and a hint of admiration, though she quickly glanced at Dae-hyun, careful not to let her words sting.

Before Joon-ho could answer, Valentina leaned in with a mischievous grin. "Forget movies—Dae-hyun must have stepped out of Crash Landing on You. He's giving me Major Pyo Chi-su vibes. Inspector Wong? He doesn't belong here. He's overdue for a lead role in Bridgerton.""

The group froze, turning to Valentina in collective surprise.

"What?" she said defensively, her cheeks flushing slightly. "Camila's love for Korea rubbed off on me, okay? Netflix is a dangerous thing. If they don't put Inspector Wong in a Regency coat soon, they're wasting his potential."

Dae-hyun threw up his hands in mock outrage. "Wait, wait—he gets Bridgerton, and I get Pyo Chi-su? This is an outrage."

Dae-hyun groaned dramatically. "Pyo Chi-su? Really? I'm way cooler than that g uy."

Valentina smirked. "Sure, keep telling yourself that."

Camila chuckled, throwing Valentina a playful look.

Camila ignored Dae-hyun's theatrics and turned back to Joon-ho with a raised eyebrow.

Joon-ho shrugged. "He's always been like that. Even in school, after his family moved here, people thought he was too good to be real."

Dae-hyun, however, wasn't letting it go. "You didn't tell me you called him!" he accused Joon-ho. "You know Jen hates me. What if she came instead?"

"Let's move on before Jen tracks us down too," Joon-ho said, turning to lead the group toward the next leg of their adventure.

Chapter 16: To begin is to win half the fight; what am I?

The group's journey along the Path of Five Virtues had come to an end, but the echoes of their adventure lingered as they returned to Seoul. The artifacts were safely in the care of the National Museum, their stories preserved for future generations. Yet, the thrill of the chase, the bonds they'd formed, and the unexpected twists kept their minds racing long after the final artifact was secured.

They gathered at a small restaurant near the museum, the warm glow of lanterns reflecting on the wooden tables as they toasted their success. The scent of sizzling meat and spices filled the air, a comforting contrast to the tension that had marked their journey.

"To the Path," Joon-ho said, raising his glass.

"To teamwork ," Camila added with a smile.

"To snacks and rubber chickens," Dae-hyun chimed in, earning a round of laughter.

"And to unexpected adventures," Valentina said, her tone softer but sincere.

Dae-hyun glanced at his phone and saw a weird headline on Naver. As he clicked on a trending video, he nearly choked on his dried squid snack.

The title read: "**Karma Strikes Treasure-Hunting Trio and Disgraced Tour Guide.**"

The shaky footage showed a familiar group of disheveled faces—two short men and a tall man, the treasure-seeking trio they had been dealing with. The narrator described how their unauthorized excavation attempts at a heritage site had gone disastrously wrong.

"...and their so-called guide, a man once known for running local tours, was apprehended for trespassing and illegal artifact handling," the news anchor stated. The video cut to the shifty tour guide, his face pale and clearly panicked, as authorities escorted him away.

Dae-hyun leaned back, laughing so hard his chair nearly tipped over.

As the night wore on, Joon-ho's phone buzzed with a message from Professor Choi. His brow furrowed as he read it, then broke into a rare smile.

"What is it?" Camila asked, leaning closer.

"The museum is planning an exhibition on the Path of Five Vir tues," Joon-ho replied. "They want us to be part of the opening event. Apparently, our work is being recognized as one of the most significant historical discoveries of the decade."

Dae-hyun leaned back, grinning. "Finally, the fame I deser ve."

Valentina smirked. "You deserve? Pretty sure it was a group effor t."

"Details," Dae-hyun said, waving a hand dismissively. "The point is, my face will be on the posters, right?"

Dae-hyun's excitement only grew as he began sketching out grandiose plans for their newfound fame.

"We could do a world tour," he suggested. "Live reenactments of the journey. I'll play myself, obviously."

Camila rolled her eyes. "And who would play the rest of us?"

"Don't worry, I'll cast appropriately," Dae-hyun said with mock seriousness. "Valentina, you'll get someone brooding and intense. Camila, someone charming yet feisty. Joon-ho, someone with, uh, good handwriting?"

Joon-ho sighed, but a faint smile tugged at his lips. "Let's focus on the exhibition first."

The air grew quieter as the group stepped outside, drawn to the lantern-lit street.

Dae-hyun caught Valentina's attention, his usual humor replaced by something more serious. "Hey, Valentina," he began, his voice unusually soft.

She turned, eyebrows raised. "What now, Chicken Man?"

"I've been thinking," he said, hesitating for once. "You've put up with my antics this whole time, and... well, you've got this way of calling me out and keeping me grounded."

Valentina smirked. "It's a full-time job."

Dae-hyun chuckled, then met her gaze. "I'm serious. I think... I'm in love with you."

Camila said Joon-ho stopped so suddenly, they almost stopped breathing.

Camila looked back and forth at Dae-hyun and Valentina, unsure if she should even acknowledge the moment. Joon-ho took her by the forearm and swiftly whisked her away from the couple.

Valentina's smirk faltered, replaced by something softer. "You're serious?"

Dae-hyun nodded, his usual grin fading into vulnerability.

Valentina stepped closer, her voice quieter. "You're a lot to handle, Chicken Man. But... I like it."

Dae-hyun's grin returned, lighting up his face. "Does that mean I'm not completely out?"

"Don't push your luck ," Valentina said, her tone light but affectionate.

On the other side of the street, Joon-ho stood beside Camila, his hands tucked into his pockets.

"You've been quiet," Camila said, tilting her head to look at him.

"I've been thinking," Joon-ho replied, his gaze distant. "About how much I admire your courage. Your curiosity. It's... inspiring."

Camila raised an eyebrow, her teasing smile softening. "Are you trying to tell me something? God, don't pull out a red umbrella or a red scarf, okay."

He glanced at her, his usual reserved demeanor faltering. "I care about you. More than I probably should."

Camila blinked, caught off guard. She opened her mouth to respond, then paused. Slowly, she reached out and gave his hand a quick squeeze.

"Good to know it wasn't just me feeling this way," she said, her voice warm.

As the night deepened, the group returned to the restaurant to finish their meal, their laughter and shared stories weaving through the warm air.

"So," Valentina said, her arms crossed. "What now?"

"The exhibition," Joon-ho said. "And then... who knows?"

"Whatever it is, it won't be boring," Camila said with a grin.

Dae-hyun raised his hand. "I vote for more snacks and fewer treasure hunters."

"Agreed, time for Netflix," Valentina said, smirking. "Let's get some ramen Chicken Man."

Dae-hyun started coughing so hard, Joon-ho stopped slapping his back for fear of his actually coughing up a lung.

Epilogue: Each end I mark is a start anew, leading you onward; what am I?

The night outside the National Museum was quiet, the earlier buzz of the exhibit's opening reduced to a faint hum as attendees trickled away.

The grand exhibition opening was a dazzling affair, drawing historians, journalists, and art enthusiasts from across the country and beyond. The main hall was alive with conversation, the soft glow of spotlights illuminating the carefully curated displays. At the center of it all, the Path of Five Virtues artifacts stood reverently behind glass, unveiled to the world for the first time. Camila and Joon-ho sat at the team's table along the exhibition wall, the attention making them slightly uncomfortable. Camila fidgeted with her napkin, while Joon-ho maintained a stoic composure, though his grip on his glass betrayed his nerves. In contrast, Valentina leaned back with a satisfied grin, basking in the accolades, while Dae-hyun gleefully waved at anyone who glanced their way, thoroughly enjoying the limelight.

No sight of any rubber chickens – so far.

Scattered across the hall were the retired historians, each seated at a table that, when viewed from above, seemed to form the five points of a crescent moon. They watched the proceedings with quiet pride. Though separated by space, their shared purpose connected them to the central table, where the team now sat, the culmination of their efforts displayed for the world to admire. Um Soo-hyun, Nam Joon-seok, Im Hye-won, Tae Ji-yoon, and Yoo Min-hee. The night felt like a tribute— not just to the artifacts, but to the enduring virtues they represented.

The group stood on the museum steps, bathed in the glow of Seoul's city lights. Their adventure had come to an end, yet an unspoken energy lingered between them, a sense that their story was far from over.

Dae-hyun, ever the comedian, had been unusually quiet, until now. His new electric blue rubber chicken now firmly in his hand. As the others chatted, he took a step closer to Valentina, his usual bravado replaced with a rare vulnerability.

"You know," he began, his voice quieter than usual, "I've been thinking. This whole journey... I didn't just do it for the fame or the snacks."

Valentina smirked, folding her arms. "Oh? Then what was it for? The chicken?"

"You," he said simply, his gaze steady for once. "You're the reason I kept going when things got tough. And maybe... the reason I'd do it all over again."

Valentina's sharp wit softened into a rare smile. "You've come a long way, Chicken Man. You're not as bad as I thought."

"Maybe badder?" he teased, his grin returning.

"Don't push it," she replied, but her tone held warmth as she stepped closer.

A few tables away, the undeniable presence of Inspector Wong and his wife, Jen, stole the room's attention. Women lingered nearby, pretending to chat while trying to catch the Inspector's eye. His rugged, K-drama/idol looks and effortless charm were impossible to ignore, and the press had wasted no time snapping candid photos of the striking couple.

Jen, however, was as formidable as she was beautiful, her uniform commanding the same respect as her husband's. A highly ranked officer in her own right, she sent a swift, pointed glance at the admiring women, her gaze sharp and unapologetic. The message was clear: Don't even think about it.

Dae-hyun caught her eye for a brief moment, and Jen smirked, tapping her phone. A second later, his phone buzzed in his pocket. When he checked, the screen read: "Behave, Dae-hyun or the rubber chicken dies."

He gulped and tucked his phone away quickly, earning a soft chuckle from Joon-ho, who had witnessed the entire exchange.

Jen leaned back into her chair with practiced ease, her hand casually resting on Wong's arm. The crowd grew uncomfortable. In a way, they knew better than to linger too long.

Sitting beside Inspector Wong was Preston Gregory, sipping his drink with the air of a man who had seen it all. The former university classmate of both Joon-ho and Wong, and longtime Korea resident, Preston was as much a part of the city's soul as the historic venues he performed in. Dressed impeccably but exuding effortless charm, his smooth dark mocha skin contrasted elegantly against the crisp lines of his tailored suit, while his lush, impeccably trimmed beard added to the effortless sophistication of his presence. He smirked as he watched Jen silently assert dominance over the entire room.

The four main guests walked over to greet the nightclub owner and two officers. Formal introductions among the friends and ladies were done.

"Ah, Dae-hyun," Preston mused, swirling his drink. "I remember when you were just a kid tagging along, dreaming about being famous. Now look at you—just as ridiculous, but in a tux."

Dae-hyun turned to him, scandalized. "I am the entertainment for the night! Have you ever seen someone handle a rubber chicken with this much finesse?"

"I have," Preston said dr yly. "Last week. At a pet store."

A few steps away, Camila and Joon-ho walked towards a quiet corner, their conversation muted under the glow of the museum's lanterns.

"You've been distant all night," Camila said, her voice laced with curiosity.

Joon-ho hesitated, his hands tucked into his pockets. "I've been reflecting," he admitted. "On everything we've done. On everything I've learned. Especially... about you."

Camila tilted her head, a small smile playing on her lips. "What about me?"

"You challenged me," Joon-ho said, meeting her gaze. "Not just as a historian, but as a person. You made me see the world differently. And... you made me want to be part of it with you."

For a moment, Camila was silent, her teasing demeanor giving way to something softer. "You're not bad for a serious historian, you know."

Joon-ho chuckled. "I'll take that as a compliment."

Camila leaned closer, her smile widening. "It is."

The tender moments were interrupted by the unmistakable sound of Dae-hyun's rubber chicken squeaking furiously.

"Not to ruin the mood," he called, holding up the chicken, "but this thing is a magnet for chaos."

Everyone at the table turned to Dae-hyun and his chicken. Valentina rolled her eyes. "What now?"

Dae-hyun gave the chicken an annoyed shake, and with an unexpected pop, something small and solid tumbled out of its hollow base and clinked onto the marble floor. Everyone froze as the object skittered a few inches before stopping—a tiny, worn velvet ring box.

Camila blinked. "Is... is that what I think it is?"

Dae-hyun's eyes widened as he bent down and picked up the box, holding it gingerly as if it might explode. "This can't be mine," he stammered. "I mean, I didn't—why was this in the chicken?"

The group leaned in closer as he slowly opened the box. Inside was a simple but elegant ring, its modest diamond sparkling faintly in the glow of the museum lights.

Valentina let out a gasp before narrowing her eyes. "Is this a joke? Dae-hyun, if you've been carrying this thing around as some elaborate prank, I'm going to—"

"It's not mine!" he interrupted, his face beet red. "I swear, I have no idea how it got in there!"

Joon-ho, standing quietly nearby, suddenly cleared his throat. His stoic demeanor cracked as a nervous smile played at the edges of his lips. "Actually... it's mine."

The group turned to him in stunned silence.

Joon-ho stepped forward, his eyes locking with Camila's. "I, uh... I didn't know when or how to... well, it's been a long journey, and I thought maybe—"

Camila, realizing what was happening, let out a soft laugh, her cheeks flushed. "Joon-ho, are you telling me you put a proposal ring in that chicken?"

"It seemed like a safe place at the time!" he blurted, his usual calm unraveling. "I didn't expect it to happen like this."

Dae-hyun fell into laughter, even Valentina doubling over as Joon-ho sheepishly grinned from ear to ear. "You've got to hand it to me Hyung," Dae-hyun said smugly. "If it weren't for my chicken, this moment wouldn't exist. You're welcome."

Joon-ho shook his head, the tension easing as he turned back to Camila. "It's not how I planned it, but... what do you think?"

Camila smiled, taking the box from his hands. "I think it's perfect," she said softly. "Yes."

The group erupted into cheers, with Dae-hyun hoisting the rubber chicken triumphantly. "This thing deserves a place in the museum!"

As the celebration continued, Preston leaned in toward Inspector Wong and Dae-hyun, his deep voice laced with amusement. "So, I assume you two will be hosting and officiating this thing?"

Inspector Wong smirked, taking a slow sip of his drink. Jen surprised everyone by interjecting.

"Only if I get to arrest Dae-hyun at the reception for public disturbance."

Preston nodded solemnly. "And I'll be warming up for the inevitable love ballads. Let me guess—something grand, something timeless, something that'll make the aunts cry. Probably Love Wins All, right?"

Dae-hyun, never one to miss an opportunity, leaned in with a mischievous grin. "Great choice, hyung. But, hear me out—why not Love, Money, Fame instead?"

Preston arched a brow. "A Seventeen song? About the chaotic pitfalls of relationships? At a wedding?"

Dae-hyun shrugged. "I'm just saying, it sets the right expectations. Love is great and all, but throw in some fame, a bit of money, and suddenly you've got plot twists. Keep it real, you know?"

Preston sighed, shaking his head. "Yeah, nothing says romance like a satirical take on modern relationships. Maybe I'll perform both—start with IU, end with pure irony."

Dae-hyun snapped his fingers. "Now **that's** a setlist. You get them soft first, then hit them with the reality check."

Valentina, having reached her limit. "Or—
and I cannot stress this enough—you
could just let the couple enjoy their
moment without turning it into a variety
show."

Dae-hyun gasped in faux offense. "You
wound me."

She gave him a dry look. "Not yet."

And with that, the celebration carried on,
leaving Preston shaking his head and
muttering something about why does he
still put up with Dae-hyun after all these
years.

He turns to Joon-ho and pats him on the
back.

"This better be an open bar bro."

Joon-ho chuckled, the weight of the
moment sinking in.

And as the celebration continued inside, the artifacts sat safely, and along with the Guardians, watching over a moment not scripted in legend, but born from the very virtues they had uncovered together.

THE END?

Don't be too sure...

Riddles and Wisdom: Unveiling the Idioms

Each chapter begins with a riddle because life, like a great mystery, thrives on curiosity and discovery. These riddles are not mere puzzles; they are the keys to understanding deeper truths hidden within the journey of the stor y.

Like the characters navigating Seoul's intricate streets, the reader is invited to embark on their own quest—unraveling each riddle to reveal an idiom steeped in cultural wisdom.

These idioms, like treasures, carry profound meaning, reminding us that every challenge we face is a doorway to growth, every connection we make is a bridge to understanding, and every moment of reflection is a gift.

By the time the book ends, the riddles will not just be solved; they will become tools of insight, small treasures carried forward into your own life's journey.

Enjoy!

"Shining bright, yet beneath me, secrets hide in plain sight; what am I?"

" 등 잔 밑 이 어 둡 다 " (Deungjan mit-i eodupda) - "It is darkest under the lamp."

Meaning: Hidden truths are often found in plain sight.

"Speak with kindness, and kindness returns; what am I?"
" 가 는 말 이 고 와 야 오 는 말 이 곱 다 "
(Ganeun mal-i gowaya oneun mal-i gopda) - "If the outgoing words are beautiful, the incoming words will be beautiful too."
Meaning: Respectful and kind words foster positive relationships.

Chapter 2: Many, Yet Nothing Until Strung Together

"Though I'm many, I am nothing until strung together; what am I?"

"구슬이 서 말이라도 꿰어야 보배다"

(Guseul-i seo mal-irado kkweoya bobae-da) - "Even if you have a pile of jewels, you need to string them together to make a treasure."

Meaning: Collaboration or effort is required to create value.

Chapter 3: Through Struggle, I Bring Joy

"Through struggle I grow, and at the end, I bring joy; what am I?"

"고생 끝에 낙이 온다" (Gosaeng kkeut-e naki onda) - "At the end of hardship comes happiness."

Meaning: Perseverance through struggles leads to rewards.

Chapter 4: Small, Yet Enough of Me Can Build Mountains

"Though I am small, gather enough of me, and I will rise; what am I?"
"티끌 모아 태산" (Tikkeul moa taesan) - "Dust gathers to make a mountain."
Meaning: Small efforts accumulate into great achievements.

Chapter 5: Even When Skies Fall, I Show the Way

"Even when the skies fall, I show you a way out; what am I?"
"하늘이 무너져도 솟아날 구멍이 있다" (Haneul-i muneojyeodo sotanal gumeong-i itda) - "Even if the sky falls, there is a hole to escape through."
Meaning: There is always hope and a solution, no matter the difficulty.

Chapter 6: Mix Me Into Myself, I Remain Unchanged

"Mix me into myself, and you will find no change; what am I?"

"물에 물 탄 듯 술에 술 탄 듯" (Mul-e mul tan deut sul-e sul tan deut) - "Like water added to water, like alcohol added to alcohol."

Meaning: Blending identical things makes no difference.

"Speak my name, and you might see me appear; what am I?"

"호랑이도 제 말 하면 온다" (Horangi-do je mal hamyeon onda) - "Even a tiger will come if you talk about it."

Meaning: Mentioning something often attracts its presence.

Chapter 8: From a Stream, I Rise to Touch the Skies

"From a humble stream, I rise to touch the skies; what am I?"
"개천에서 용 난다" (Gaecheon-eseo yong nanda) - "A dragon rises from a small stream."
Meaning: Greatness can emerge from humble beginnings.

Chapter 9: Unplanned, Catching You Unaware

"I come unplanned, catching you unaware; what am I?"

" 가 는 날 이 장 날 이 다 " (Ganeun nal-i jangnal-ida) - "The day you go is the market day."

Meaning: Unexpected situations often arise at the most inconvenient times.

Chapter 10: Alone I'm Heavy, But With Help I Am Light

"Alone I'm heavy, but with help, I'm light; what am I?"

" 백 지 장 도 맞 들 면 낫 다 "

(Baekjijangdo
matdeulmyeon natda) - "Even a sheet of paper is lighter when lifted together."
Meaning: Teamwork makes any task easier.

Chapter 11: I Always Know, Whether Sun Shines or Moon Glows

"What's said in secret, I always know, whether sun shines or moonlight glows; what am I?"

"낮말은 새가 듣고 밤말은 쥐가 듣는다" (Najmal-eun saega deutgo bam-mal-eun juiga deutneunda) - "The birds hear what you say during the day, and the mice hear what you say at night."

Meaning: Be cautious with words; they can always be overheard.

Chapter 12: Patience and Persistence Will Yield

"With patience and persistence, even the strongest will yield; what am I?"

"열 번 찍어 안 넘어가는 나무 없다" (Yeol beon jjigeo an neomeoganeun namu eopda) - "No tree will remain standing after being struck ten times."

Meaning: Persistence overcomes all obstacles.

Chapter 13: Longer Roads Hold the Greatest Tales

"The longer the road, the more tales I hold; what am I?"

"가는 길이 멀어야 말이 많다" (Ganeun gili meol-eoya mal-i manta) - "The longer the journey, the more stories there are to tell."

Meaning: Challenges enrich the narrative and create meaning.

"Hear me a hundred times, but see me once to truly know; what am I?"

"백 번 듣는 것이 한 번 보는 것만 못하다" (Baek beon deudneun geos-i han beon boneun geos-man mot-hada) - "Hearing something a hundred times is not as good as seeing it once."

Meaning: Firsthand experience is more valuable than hearsay.

Chapter 15: Good Endings Make All Worthwhile

"No matter the struggle, my good end will make all worthwhile; what am I?"

"끝이 좋아야 다 좋다" (Kkeut-i joaya da jota) - "If the ending is good, everything is good."

Meaning: A satisfying conclusion makes the journey worthwhile.

Chapter 16: The Start of All Triumphs

"To begin is to win half the fight; what am I?"

"시작이 반이다" (Sijagi ban-ida) - "Starting is half the battle."

Meaning: The hardest part of any task is taking the first step; progress flows naturally from there.

Epilogue: Ends Mark New Beginnings

"Each end I mark is a start anew, leading you onward; what am I?"

"산 넘어 산" (San neomeo san) - "Over the mountain is another mountain."

Meaning: Every ending leads to new challenges and new opportunities.

To this I say... until we meet again.

Em

About Margins Abound LLC

Some stories arrive quietly, tapping at the edges of what we think we know.

Others break through, demanding a place on the page.

Margins Abound was created for both kinds—

for the dreamers, wanderers, and wordsmiths who live between worlds, and for readers who recognize themselves in the in-between.

Every book we publish begins with wonder and ends with connection. Some make you laugh. Some make you ache. All of them make you feel alive.

Visit www.marginsabound.com and follow the threads of imagination wherever they lead.

About the Author

Em Green writes cross-cultural fiction that mixes curiosity, heart, and humor. Her stories explore what it means to connect — across distance, language, and expectation — and to rediscover ourselves in unfamiliar places.

When she isn't writing, she's probably wandering through libraries, sketching story ideas on napkins, or researching the tiny details that make worlds feel real. Em believes every place has a rhythm and every person a story waiting to be heard.

You can find all of her books and current projects at www.marginsabound.com

More from Em Green

A Seoul Searching Adventure is just the beginning.

If you enjoyed the twists, humor, and heart found in this story, you'll want to explore The Rating Game Book Series, co-created and co-written by Em Green and local Utah author Sean O'Leary.

Books 1-4 are already available:**RatingGameBooks.com**

Book 1: Illusions of Perfection

Book 2: Chasing Stars

Book 3: The Ultimate Price

Books 4: Unbound: The Final Rating

And as for Book 5? Special Edition readers may be the first to see it.

All Special Editions of The Rating Game will be made available through Margins Abound LLC, while the original versions are published by Sean O'Leary Books LLC and are available at RatingGameBooks.com.

♀ Follow upcoming releases and announcements at:

☞ MarginsAbound.com

www.ingramcontent.com/pod-product-compliance
Lightning Source LLC
Chambersburg PA
CBHW051636260626
47170CB00004B/1196